WITHDRAWN

WING & CLAW

CAVERN OF SECRETS

ALSO BY LINDA SUE PARK

NOVELS

Wing & Claw: Forest of Wonders

Seesaw Girl

The Kite Fighters

A Single Shard

When My Name Was Keoko

Project Mulberry

Archer's Quest

Keeping Score

The 39 Clues: Storm Warning

A Long Walk to Water

The 39 Clues: Trust No One

PICTURE BOOKS

Yaks Yak!

The Firekeeper's Son

Mung-Mung

What Does Bunny See?

Yum! Yuck!

Tap Dancing on the Roof

Bee-bim Bop!

The Third Gift

Xander's Panda Party

LINDA SUE PARK

WING & CLAW

CAVERN OF SECRETS

ILLUSTRATED BY
JAMES MADSEN

HARPER
An Imprint of HarperCollinsPublishers

HarperCollins
PUBLISHERS
Since 1817

Wing & Claw #2: Cavern of Secrets

ISBN 978-0-06-232741-3

Typography by Joe Merkel
Map by Mike Schley
17 18 19 20 21   CG/LSCH   10 9 8 7 6 5 4 3 2 1
❖
First Edition

To Callan

The Vast

Shed
Compound
Stables
Northern
Slums
Northern
Ferry
Landing
Forest of
Wonders
The Commons
Chancellery
Garrison
Apothecary
Quarter
Everwide River
Farmsteads
The Mag
Raffa's
Home
Pother
Settlement

The Vast

PART 1

CHAPTER ONE

T HE wind stirred the green needles of the never-bare trees. They swayed and leaned toward each other, murmuring of the coming spring.

The trees surrounded the entrance to a cave, which was partially blocked by a huge lichen-covered boulder. Or perhaps it was a pile of dried bracken, for it, too, trembled in the wind.

Then the pile began to stretch and shift, taking on a more distinct shape. A shaggy head . . . an enormous torso . . .

The gigantic golden bear seemed to be emerging from the mountain itself. Rising to her full height, she opened her mouth and growled, a low rumble that grew into a throaty roar.

Raffa was woken by thunder.

Odd upon strange, he thought. A thunderstorm at this time of year? He rubbed his eyes and saw Kuma sitting up on her pallet.

"That's her—she's awake!" Kuma exclaimed in delight, and jumped to her feet.

As Raffa followed her out of the shelter, he marveled at the thought of a bear so big that he'd mistaken her growl for thunder.

They stopped just short of the mouth of the cave. The bear stood on her hind legs, half again as tall as a man, and sniffed the air for several seconds. Back down on all fours, she shook herself so hard that fur flew like snow, then retreated a few steps deeper into the cave.

Raffa could see joy and relief on Kuma's face. It was one thing to know that bears hibernate. It was quite another for Kuma to have seen her beloved Roo breathing so infrequently for these many weeks that it almost seemed as if she had forgotten how.

Moments of joy had been all but absent for Raffa's little group that winter. Months earlier, they had fled

Gilden and escaped to the desolate wilderness of the Sudden Mountains. There, they had spent the daylight hours focused entirely on two activities: keeping warm and finding food. The work was too hard, the wind too cold, the snow too deep. There was never enough to eat.

Two days ago, the wind had changed. Its knife-edged sharpness had dulled, then softened. Raffa had almost cried with relief over the shift in the weather. Since then, Kuma had been checking the cave obsessively to see if Roo was awake.

Now Raffa hung back while Kuma entered the cave. She moved slowly and spoke in a soothing tone as she approached the bear. Squatting down in front of Roo, she made herself small and unthreatening, and let Roo sniff at her.

Roo whined and swatted Kuma's shoulder affectionately with an enormous paw. Kuma was ready for this and had braced herself; otherwise, Roo's exuberant greeting might have knocked her over. Then the bear turned away and began nosing at something on the ground.

Something gray and furry, with a striped tail.

The mound of fur did not respond at first, but Roo let out a plaintive growl and persisted, continuing to nudge with her nose.

Finally, there was a mewl of protest, and the masked face of a young raccoon appeared. Twig unfurled herself, sat up, and blinked a few times, her eyes glowing purple.

"Ter-tee wah," she squeaked. "Tertee, grrrr-rum, tertee."

"She's thirsty—she wants water," said Kuma, who almost always understood Twig immediately.

Twig had gained the ability to speak after being treated with an infusion that contained a mysterious scarlet vine from the Forest of Wonders. But she could not speak nearly as well as Echo the bat, who had received the same treatment. Twig's speech was limited to a word or two at a time, interspersed with an assortment of growls, chuffs, and snorts. Raffa thought this was because she was almost always with Roo, whereas Echo spent most of his time with humans.

Raffa smiled at the little raccoon and went to fetch a strawful of melted snow for her. Following Kuma's example, he squatted down and moved slowly, while Roo kept her eye on him.

During the escape from Gilden, Twig had become separated from Bando, her twin brother, and their mother. Fortunately, Roo had taken to the little raccoon at once, and they had bonded like mother and cub. The bear tolerated Raffa and his cousin, Garith—the third human in their party—because she knew that Kuma was fond of them. Still, she never let anyone except Kuma touch her, which was fine with Raffa, who much preferred to stay a safe distance away.

Raffa gave Twig a drink. When she was finished, she pawed at the bear, who seemed fully awake and reoriented now. Roo relaxed, sat down, and allowed Kuma to scratch her with a stick. At the same time, she began giving Twig a tongue-bath.

The girl scratching the bear grooming the raccoon . . . Seeing the three of them together, Raffa felt a sharp pang of longing for his own special companion.

He made his way to the back corner of the cave. A tiny bat hung there, on a perch made out of a twig tied to a leather cord. Raffa blew on the bat's whiskers. Echo stirred, then produced an annoyed click.

Raffa tried again, blowing a little harder.

Another click, this one weaker than the first.

Raffa frowned. Neither Twig nor Echo were true hibernators like Roo, but both had slept for days at a time throughout the winter. Raffa didn't know if it was normal for bats to emerge from torpor later than raccoons. Carefully he donned the perch necklace; perhaps the warmth of his body would help Echo waken.

Echo hadn't spoken for weeks. How Raffa missed their conversations! The bat never failed to make him laugh. He could hardly wait for Echo to talk again, for then it would truly be spring, a farewell forever to this harsh winter of too little laughter.

Garith was sitting partway up inside the shelter. He had been woken not by the bear's growls but by a shaft of sunlight piercing the screen of branches.

"Garith." Raffa waved his hand to get his cousin's attention. "Roo—and—Twig—are a-wake. Want—to—go—see—them?" He spoke slowly, enunciating each syllable as clearly as he could, and making exaggerated gestures.

"I've told you before, that doesn't help!" Garith said. "Stop talking to me like I'm some kind of idiot. I lost my *hearing*, not my brain."

His voice was often a little too loud since he had become deaf. Raffa should have been used to it by now, but every reminder of Garith's deafness twisted his insides—because it was his fault. Maybe not directly, but the fact remained that Garith wouldn't be deaf if it hadn't been for Raffa's decision to flee Gilden.

Raffa had spent the winter months trying to make it up to Garith, by helping with his share of the work. But Garith resented that, too, and Raffa felt as if he were always tiptoeing around his cousin's bad moods.

Garith yanked his hood up over his head and lay down again. "Go away," he said.

His anger was more than worrisome, and for the hundredth time Raffa wished he could talk to his parents about it. But he couldn't risk going home, for none of them had any idea what awaited them there. Were their families being watched? Would neighbors turn them in? Would guards seize them the instant they were sighted?

Raffa, Kuma, and Garith could hardly be considered enemies of Obsidia. But Chancellor Leeds viewed them as a threat, for she knew that they possessed something more important than strength or power.

Knowledge.

The trio had discovered hundreds of animals trapped in a compound, where they were being dosed and trained against their natures. The Chancellor was keeping the project a secret from all but a favored few; Raffa had been one of them, for a short time. Now he was sure that she was seeking a way to silence him. He had nightmare visions of being thrown into the underground cells of the

Garrison, left to a life not worth living among the rats and the filth and the loneliness.

And the Chancellor wanted one thing even more than his silence: Roo. Raffa would never forget the shrill fervor in her voice during their escape, when she had screamed for the guards to recapture the bear. He had heard only dark and murky whispers of her plans, but he did know that she wanted to use the great bear as a weapon. Bears were rare in Obsidia, and bears the size of Roo rarer still: Keeping Roo out of the Chancellor's reach was the main reason Raffa and his friends had chosen to hide in the Suddens.

With spring finally banishing the ice and snow, Raffa found himself in an agony of indecision.

They couldn't stay here forever, but they couldn't go home, either.

Raffa slept poorly that night, waking several times to check on Echo. The next morning, the bat seemed even more inert. Raffa could see that Echo was still breathing, but his tiny body was barely warm to the touch.

He showed the bat to Kuma. "I don't know what's wrong," he said. "He should at least be starting to wake by now."

Kuma examined Echo. "Yes, I think so, too," she said slowly. "I'm sure that I've seen bats flying around in early spring."

Raffa's alarm was growing by the moment. He scolded himself silently: Panicking would do Echo no good. He thought of his parents, Mohan and Salima. When they were treating patients, they were almost always calm and deliberate. Sometimes decisions had to be made quickly. Sometimes their actions were urgent. But they were never panicky.

Think the way they would. Like an apothecary.

Pulse slow and weak . . . unresponsive to stimulus . . . torpor that no longer seemed natural. Because Raffa did not know exactly what was wrong with Echo, any treatment he used would have to be mild—one sure to do no harm.

A restorative tonic, then. He had only a few botanical supplies with him, and no equipment other than his trusty mortar and pestle. He set about grinding some anjella root, then combined it with dried mellia and wortjon.

Three times a day over the course of the next two days, Raffa dosed the bat with the combination. He checked on him constantly, even massaging Echo's tiny back in an attempt to improve his circulation.

All to no avail. If anything, the bat was worse off, for no matter how many times Raffa blew on his whiskers, Echo did not respond.

Raffa made the same infusion again, but this time he added a powder made of the stems and leaves of the scarlet vine. He had taken the entire stock of the vine from Uncle Ansel's glasshouse in Gilden, and had dried the plants to store them.

Unlike the fresh vine, the dry powder emitted not a single spark or gleam when combined with other ingredients. Raffa concentrated hard while making the infusion, but nothing came to him—no moment of color or music, no prick of discomfort. No sign at all from his intuition.

As he held the reed that contained a dose of the infusion, he hesitated. What was he to think of this blankness? Was it possible that he was losing his gift? It made him feel frightened and uncertain to have to rely solely on his training and experience. Did other apothecaries have to do that all the time?

He took a deep breath, gritted his teeth, and dosed Echo with the infusion.

The next few hours dragged by so slowly that it felt

to Raffa as if the sun had come to a standstill. He looked down the neck of his tunic every few moments, hoping to detect even the smallest change in Echo's condition.

Nothing.

The bat remained as he was, limp except for the tiny claws closed tightly around the twig.

Raffa's relief that the infusion seemed to have done no harm was overwhelmed by the harsh disappointment that it had done no good, either. He went to Kuma and Garith, fighting back tears.

"I don't know what else to do," he said, the little bat cradled in his hands. "He should be awake by now, but nothing's working."

"What?" Garith said. "What's working?" He was staring hard at Raffa's face, and Raffa realized that his cousin was trying to read his lips.

Raffa shook his head. "*Not* working," he repeated.

Garith glanced down at Echo. "You need more botanicals," he said. "It's still too cold up here—nothing's growing."

"And maybe . . ." Kuma's voice was soft with sympathy. "Maybe you could use some help—somebody to talk to about what else you could try."

Raffa swallowed past the lump in his throat and put

his hand protectively over the wee bat. Months earlier, he had saved Echo's life. Somehow that gave him a solemn responsibility for the bat. He hadn't failed Echo the first time. He couldn't fail him now.

He clenched and unclenched his jaw. Garith and Kuma were both right, and he was sure upon certain about what he had to do. When he spoke, the words came out fiercely.

"We're going home," he said.

Neither Garith nor Kuma uttered a single protest. They were well aware of the risks; at the same time, Raffa knew that each had reasons for wanting to leave the Suddens. Kuma needed to find a safe place for Roo, somewhere close enough to visit occasionally. And Garith had to go back to face his father, a meeting that Raffa suspected was both yearned for and dreaded.

"All right, then," Raffa said. "We'll leave tomorrow at daybirth."

He glanced down at Echo on the perch around his neck. "I'll get there as fast as I can, I promise," he murmured.

Ford the Everwide . . . find a hideout for Roo . . . and then go home, where—as long as no guards awaited him—there would be plenty of botanicals to work with.

Even more important, his parents would be there. Mohan, with his profound knowledge of garden botanicals, and Salima, so familiar with wild plants; both of them having years of experience treating illness and injury. Surely, with their help, he could cure the little bat.

Then Raffa's stomach lurched at his next thought.

If only Echo lives long enough to get there.

CHAPTER TWO

A S they broke camp, the threesome discussed the route. They had felt safe in the Suddens, believing the terrain to be too remote and too vast for the Chancellor's guards to search, and indeed, there had been no sign of pursuit that winter.

But heading for home would bring them closer to Gilden—and to the risk of being recaptured.

"We need to ford the river here in the mountains," Raffa said. He made snaking motions with his hands toward Garith. "Near its source." Only there would the Everwide River be narrow enough to cross without a boat or a raft.

"But how will we find it?" Kuma asked.

Garith was glancing from his face to Kuma's, his eyes narrowed in concentration. With a pang, Raffa realized how hard it must be to follow a conversation by reading lips.

"The source?" Garith said, looking at their faces for confirmation. "Da was there once. He told me about it. It starts near the peak closest to the Southern Woodlands."

There was a brief, uncomfortable silence, as there always was when Garith's father, Ansel, was mentioned. None of them could ever forget Ansel's decision to send the screaming owl to stop Raffa and Kuma from escaping with Roo. It was an act of betrayal so agonizing that Raffa tried to keep it shut away in a far dark corner of his mind.

And it had to be even worse for Garith. By helping Raffa escape, Garith had in a single act estranged himself from his father.

Raffa avoided eye contact with his cousin as he shouldered his rucksack, regretting its near-emptiness. He had escaped from Gilden with a decent store of botanicals, but nearly all of them had been used up over the winter to treat coughs and colds, cuts and chilblains. The rucksack now held only a few powders, his waterskin, some rags, and a lightstick.

Over one shoulder, he wore his leather rope in a loose coil. He had made the rope himself by cutting up the fine tunic sewn for him by his mother. Salima had been more disappointed than angry, which he regretted, for he hated displeasing her. But the rope had proved its usefulness, and he was never without it.

He took one last look around at the site that had been home for the last few months.

No, he thought, that wasn't quite right.

It had been a shelter, not a home.

An unusual procession struck out down the mountainside. Kuma took the lead, walking stick in hand. She was followed by Roo. The bear was on all fours and wore a most decorative headpiece: Twig, clinging to Roo's ears, her striped tail curled neatly around the bear's forehead.

"Up *snuffle snuffle*," Twig chirruped happily. "Up *snuffle snork!*"

Garith was next, and Raffa was last in line, with Echo on the perch necklace.

Raffa hadn't realized before how dependent he had become on Echo's scouting. Months earlier, when the group left Gilden and made their way into the Suddens, Echo had constantly made forays into the air and reported back to Raffa. More than once, his squeaks and clicks of alarm had directed the group away from dangerous crevasses. Without the bat's guidance, Raffa felt as if they were walking blind.

He checked on Echo constantly. It seemed that with every step he took, his worry for the little bat grew. He struggled to smother his darkest thoughts. *What if . . . what if we don't make it home in time?*

Over six grueling days, they hiked down one mountain and up and over the next. The going was slower than slow; they moved a step at a time, fearful of the treacherous terrain. They had to stop each day well before sunfall to find shelter and gather firewood. In their makeshift camps, the nights were cold and miserable; the lack of sleep exhausted them, delaying their progress still further.

Raffa found himself thinking of the people who had traveled through the Suddens to reach Obsidia, including his own ancestors on his father's side. The groups of people known as the Afters—because of their arrival after the Great Quake—had crossed the entire range, a trip so perilous that more had perished than survived. No matter where the Afters came from, they would have had to scale a dozen or more peaks. He marveled now at their courage and determination.

At last the rugged terrain eased into rolling hills. For two days they traversed the foothills, where the snow was only ankle-deep, a relief from the hip-high drifts in the peaks. Midmorning of the third day, Kuma called out that she could see the beginnings of the Southern Woodlands. They continued hiking until they came to the Everwide.

Snowmelt had turned its flow into a boiling, foaming torrent. To the group's disappointment, the river at this point was too wide to cross. Reluctantly, they turned back toward the mountains and began climbing again. They followed the riverbank upward but had to diverge from it often when their path was blocked by overgrowth or downed trees or snowdrifts.

A little after sunpeak, Roo raised herself to her hind legs and bellowed. She plunged into the river, with Twig hanging on for dear life. Two-thirds of the way across, Roo scrabbled about in the current for a few moments. Then she crossed to the far side with a large trout in her mouth.

The three humans watched Roo chomp away at the trout until only the piece closest to the tail remained. Then she reached up and pulled Twig off her head, as if the raccoon were a hat. She set Twig down on the ground and gave her the fishtail.

The raccoon took the tidbit to the water's edge, washed it thoroughly, and ate it with obvious enjoyment.

Kuma clapped her hands, laughing, and Raffa had to join in. Even Garith smiled.

"It's a sign," Kuma said. "We should ford here."

Roo's crossing had shown them that the river at this point was no deeper than her chest. Raffa studied the water. The current was swift, but there were no foaming rapids.

Plate-sized chunks of ice floated past. Raffa scrambled back onto the bank for a better view. Upriver, he could see patches of white where the snow had not yet melted, indicating sheets of ice beneath.

He rejoined his companions. "It's as good a place as any," he said. "Farther up, there are ice patches, but they don't look like they'd bear our weight."

He held his coiled leather rope out to Kuma. "If you could call Roo back and tie this around her," he said, "we can use it to guide ourselves across."

Kuma put her hands behind her back.

"Tie her up? I'd never do that," she said indignantly. "She's not some kind of—of performing bear."

Raffa scowled. "I know that. It wouldn't be like tying her up to . . . restrain her or anything."

For response, Kuma pressed her lips together into a straight line.

Raffa glanced at the river. It might be possible to ford without the rope, but he wouldn't want to risk it—not for himself or any of the others.

At that moment, he realized with surprise that ever since the decision to leave the Suddens, he had been acting as if he were the group's leader.

He had never meant for that to happen. Throughout the winter, it was Kuma who had taken the lead, with her greater experience at living in the wild. Raffa had been glad to follow her instructions on how to build the shelter, weave baskets, string fish to dry. And before that, in what now seemed like another life, Raffa had always shadowed Garith, who was a year older and a head taller.

But Garith was no longer himself. And Kuma, it seemed, was now thinking of nothing other than Roo. Raffa usually admired her commitment to the well-being of animals, but sometimes—

Animals . . . That was the answer. Kuma's strength and weakness.

Raffa looked into her eyes and spoke in a voice both earnest and pleading. "Kuma, we have to get across. It would be safer using the rope, and quicker, too, and I need to get Echo home as soon as I can."

He saw her gaze flick to his neckline; Echo was tucked away, out of sight under his tunic. Then she sighed, and he knew that her innate kindness to all beasts and creatures had won out.

"Just this once," she said.

Kuma whistled for Roo, who loped back through the icy water. It took Kuma a few tries before she was able to tie the rope around the bear's massive waist. Roo let out a growl and pawed at the leather.

"It's only for a few minutes, Roo, okay?" Kuma said.

At Raffa's request, she also tied the rucksack around Roo's neck. It now contained Echo on the perch necklace, wrapped carefully in soft rags.

Kuma sent Roo to the far side again. When the bear turned and looked at her, Kuma held up both hands in a "stop" gesture. Roo planted all four of her massive paws firmly on the ground.

Because of the length necessary to circle Roo's waist, the remaining rope did not reach all the way across the river. Holding the other end, Raffa and Garith gritted their teeth and stood knee-deep in the freezing water at the edge. With one hand on the rope, Kuma waded into the current. She moved hand over hand, reaching the halfway point easily.

"It's p-p-pretty s-s-slippery," she called out, her teeth chattering.

As if to prove her point, she lost her footing and almost went under. But she hauled herself back up using the rope, with both boys bracing themselves against her weight. On the other side, Roo moaned a little but moved not a hair, while Twig watched intently, chittering in concern.

Kuma crossed to the other side without further mishap. She crouched down and hugged her knees, trying to warm herself.

Raffa put a hand on his cousin's arm. "Wait," he said. Knowing that he would be holding Garith's weight on his own from this end, he wrapped the rope twice around his wrist.

Garith started across. Strong and athletic, he made rapid progress to the middle of the river, where he stopped to look at Raffa over his shoulder. He waved, signaling that all was well.

Then a thunderous *crack* splintered the air. Raffa jerked his head in the direction of the sound.

Upstream, a huge plate of ice had broken away. It caught the current and was now hurtling directly toward Garith. In the next second, realization struck Raffa like a blow.

Garith wouldn't have heard the noise.

If he had, he could have hurried and made it across before the floe reached him. But he was just beginning to move again, and with his eyes on the water in front of him, he didn't see Kuma gesturing frantically on the far side.

Raffa did the only thing he could think of to get Garith's attention: He gave the rope a tug.

It was a disastrous mistake. The rope jerked out of Garith's hands. As he flailed his arms trying to grab it, the floe slammed into his legs. He toppled into the water, where the current snatched him and pulled him under the ice.

"GARITH!" Kuma screamed in horror.

Raffa took a single giant step, then dove.

It was so cold that his breath seemed to freeze solid in his lungs. His eyes were open, but he saw only blackness, the unspeakable cold numbing his brain. Instinctively, he surfaced, every muscle and nerve in his body pushing him upward.

Forcing another breath into his paralyzed lungs, Raffa ducked under again. He focused his entire being on a single thought: *Find Garith!* He kicked his legs and tried to make swimming motions with his arms, which felt like they were made of wood.

Through the fog of his vision, he saw a shadow to his right and made a desperate grab for it. Was it a branch or—or—

It was Garith's forearm!

Raffa's fingers closed around it. He gripped it with all his might. Hardly knowing what he was doing, he yanked his cousin out from under the floe.

Both their heads emerged. Raffa could no longer feel his limbs. He took a strangled, choking mouthful of air as he slipped on the rocky riverbed. Unable to regain his balance, he fell back into the water. With no strength left to fight the cold and the current, he was dragged beneath the ice.

A raging red cloud filled his brain and blotted out all thought.

CHAPTER THREE

RAFFA couldn't move, couldn't breathe. There was a terrible weight on his chest. On his face, too, smothering him. . . . Was this what it felt like to drown?

Odd . . . upon strange. Never knew . . . drowning . . . smells awful. So awful . . .

He tried to turn his head away from the nasty odor. From somewhere far away, he heard voices.

"Is he— It looks like he's waking up!"

"Roo, you can get off him now. Gently—"

"Raffa, wake up!"

Garith. That was Garith's voice. Did he drown, too?

With a dreadful spasm, Raffa retched several times, spitting out mouthfuls of water, then curled up on his side. Opening his eyes seemed to require as much effort as lifting a boulder.

Garith's face swam in and out of focus. Raffa fixed his gaze on Garith's nose, trying to get it to stay in one place. To his relief, it finally stopped moving. He blinked and looked into Garith's eyes.

"You scared us, you wobbler!" Garith punched his shoulder, which hurt so much that Raffa knew he wasn't dead. Relief pierced through the muddiness in his brain with the realization that Garith wasn't dead, either.

Slowly he raised himself on one elbow. Every muscle in his body twanged with pain. He saw that he was in a clearing on the riverbank, lying on a patch of dead grass.

Garith and Kuma both began talking at once.

Raffa shook his head; his brain jangled in protest. "One at a time," he croaked, and held his hand up weakly for Garith's benefit.

"Take off those wet clothes," Kuma said. "I'll get a fire going."

Raffa struggled out of his sodden boots, trousers, and undergarments, then donned his tunic again; its soft heavy wool was warm even when wet.

Shivering in muscles he didn't know he had, Raffa crouched by the fire next to Garith, who wore only his linen underclothes. In silence, they turned around from time to time, alternating roasting and freezing their fronts and backsides.

Kuma piled an armload of wood next to the fire. She spread out their wet clothes on flat stones near the flames, then plopped down beside them and stretched her toes toward the warmth.

"It was Roo. I didn't even have to say anything to her," she said proudly. "She went right into the water and dragged Garith out, and then she went back for you. Garith started coughing right away, but you were . . . I had to make you spit up some water. And you were practically frozen solid, so I got her to lie down on top of you."

So that was the smell: pure, unfiltered bear.

Then Raffa felt a little guilty for the thought. Roo couldn't help it that she smelled . . . well, like a bear. And she had just saved his life, which in all likelihood neither Kuma nor Garith could have done.

"Thank you, Roo," he said earnestly. The bear was busy grooming Twig again. Recognizing her name, she showed him her teeth in what he hoped was a smile, and

Kuma reached up to scratch her behind her ears.

"Ta-too, Roo," Twig said, imitating him. "Ta-too, *chuff chuff*, ta-too."

"It was a good thing, the rope," Kuma admitted, a little gruffly. "We pulled on it, and it led her to you, sure upon certain."

Then Raffa sat up with a jolt. "Echo!" he cried out. "What—? Where—?"

"He's here," Kuma said immediately, and brought the bat out from under her tunic. "I took him out of the rucksack to keep him warm."

"Is he—"

The look in Kuma's eyes stopped him from finishing the question. Carefully she handed over the perch necklace. Raffa cupped the little bat in one hand and placed a tense fingertip on Echo's chest.

He waited. Garith and Kuma waited with him. Even Roo and Twig were silent and still.

Please, please, please . . .

Then he felt it.

A single heartbeat.

An eternity before the next one.

Echo was closer to death than life.

* * *

Garith slumped on the ground. "It's my fault, isn't it," he said. "The ice—did it make a sound?" He looked from Raffa to Kuma and back again.

Raffa could not bring himself to answer. Kuma, stricken, gave Garith a tiny nod.

"I knew it," Garith said, and this time the bitterness in his voice was clear. "I didn't hear it, and that's why everything went wrong."

"No, Garith," Raffa said. "It was mostly my fault. I yanked on the rope—if I hadn't done that—"

But Garith wasn't looking at him. He had drawn his knees up and put his arms over his head, as if by making his body as small as possible, he could somehow disappear.

Once again, Raffa felt the familiar surge of guilt, but this time it was tangled up with anger. Garith hadn't even thanked him for pulling him out from under the ice.

Heat burned behind Raffa's eyes so fiercely that he realized his anger was not of the moment. He understood then that he'd been angry with Garith for a while now—weeks, maybe months—his ire stewing and roiling beneath the surface of his thoughts.

Because Garith's deafness *was* Raffa's fault . . . but at the same time, it wasn't. Raffa hadn't forced Garith to drink the infusion that caused his deafness; Garith had made that choice all by himself. I wasn't even *there*, Raffa thought. He clenched his jaw to keep resentful words from spewing out. The last thing he needed now was an argument with Garith.

Raffa hung Echo's perch around his neck. Then he got to his feet. His limbs still felt leaden and sore, but he forced himself to ignore the pain.

Home, he thought. Maybe not all the answers were there, but he hoped that some of them would be.

Raffa winced as he put on his clammy clothes. At least they were no longer dripping. He and Kuma tamped out the fire and scattered its remains. They waited for Garith to finish dressing, then set off again.

By midafternoon, they found themselves walking through a gorge with majestic limestone cliffs on either side. The river cut through the middle of the gorge, occasionally diverting around enormous rock formations or disappearing underground for yards at a time.

The cliffs were high, but not sheer, their faces pocked with hollows, as small as fists, as large as Roo. Hardy trees, shrubs, and vines had gained rootholds in cracks and on ledges. The vegetation was just beginning to bud out; Raffa could tell that the gorge would be cool and shady when the trees were in full leaf.

Kuma was looking around, appraising the gorge with keen interest.

"What do you think, Roo?" she asked. "Do you like it here?"

Roo sniffed the air. Like a tiny shadow of the big bear, Twig raised her head and sniffed, too.

"There's water," Raffa said, "and the caves and trees give plenty of cover. Plus it's too steep for horses. I think it would be easy for her to find places to hide if they come looking here."

He saw Kuma frown, and he added hastily, "Not that they would. I mean, it's still pretty remote."

Kuma nodded, then trotted to the base of the cliff on the left and reached for an outcrop of rock above her head. "I want to check out one of those caves," she said. "I'll only be a little while, I promise. You can go on ahead if you want. I'll catch up."

Anxious as he was to reach home and help for Echo, Raffa decided that it was a good time for a brief rest. He sat down on a handy boulder. Garith slumped to the ground with his back against the cliff. Roo, with Twig on her shoulders, began climbing in Kuma's wake. Raffa marveled at the sight of the great bear, with her bulk and weight, scaling the cliff.

"Up up up!" Twig said.

Raffa wasn't exactly afraid of climbing. But he had always thought it a more sensible choice to stay on the ground, where he couldn't fall any farther than his own height. Climb only when necessary, not for fun, please upon thank you. He shaded his eyes to watch Kuma's progress. She made scaling the cliff look easy.

The yellow and gray limestone wall was streaked thickly with white in some places, including an area not far above where he sat. Curious, Raffa stood up on the boulder to examine the white streaks more closely. As he suspected, they were droppings of some kind.

Raffa frowned and scanned the cliffs on both sides. It would take a huge flock of birds to make so many droppings. But there were no birds in sight. Where were they all?

Then he heard a tiny squeak, and at the same moment, Echo spread his wings and left the perch necklace.

"Echo!" Raffa gasped.

It was the first time in many days that the bat had made either sound or movement.

Raffa's delighted surprise vanished almost immediately: Echo was barely flying. His wings flapped
erratically; if he had been walking, Raffa would have
called it a terrible stagger. The little bat struggled a short
way up the cliff, following a heavy line of droppings.
Then he disappeared into a Y-shaped crevice.

In that instant, Raffa realized that the white streaks
were *bat* droppings. Their presence showed that a large
number of bats lived in the many caves riddling the
cliffs, and Echo had apparently sensed their proximity.
Perhaps he was seeking out his own kind—

Raffa's throat seized up with fear.

Had Echo gone into the crevice . . . to find a place
to die?

CHAPTER FOUR

RAFFA jumped down off the boulder. He hurried over to Garith, who was aimlessly scratching at the dirt with a stick.

"Echo's gone," Raffa said. He tapped Garith on the shoulder, then held up the empty perch necklace. "He went into that crack. I have to go after him." He pointed at the cliff face and mimed climbing.

"What?" Garith said with what seemed to Raffa a complete lack of interest.

"If I climb higher," Raffa said, "maybe it will, I don't know, widen out or something." His gestures were growing increasingly frantic.

Garith shrugged. "You could just wait. He might come back on his own."

"But he's so sick. What if he needs me?"

No reply.

Raffa waited a moment longer, then stomped away. He should have known that Garith wouldn't be any help.

He began climbing the cliff, doing the best he could to follow the line of the crevice into which Echo had vanished.

"Kuma!" he bellowed.

"—ooma—ooma—ooma," his voice echoed eerily between the cliffs.

"Up here," came the faint reply from far above his head.

Raffa kept as close to the cliff face as he could. At times, finding the next hand- or foothold took him many minutes; he had to move across or even down as often as up. He seemed to be progressing by inches.

Kuma called out encouragement. After the better part of an hour, he saw her peering down at him, and he hauled himself onto the broad ledge where she stood.

"It must be important," she teased, smiling. She knew how he felt about heights.

"It's Echo," he panted as he got to his feet. "He went

into the cliff—that crack there—"

Kuma's smile vanished into an expression of concern. She looked where he was pointing and scanned the cliff carefully. "Come," she said.

She grabbed his hand and pulled him toward the wall of limestone. There he saw an opening big enough for Roo to enter. Sure enough, Roo and Twig were inside, prowling around a cave perhaps five paces wide and nearly as deep. Dry and well ventilated, the cave received light and air from the opening and from holes in the walls and ceiling.

"Look," Kuma said, and pointed to a rear corner of the space.

"Look," Twig said, with a snuffle and a chuff.

Raffa walked to the corner. It was darker there. He saw another opening, this one just big enough for him to slip into if he ducked his head and turned sidewise.

"I went in, but only a little way," Kuma said. "It's a passage, and it goes toward that crack. Maybe it joins up with . . . wherever Echo went."

Raffa was already uncoiling his leather rope. He handed one end to Kuma.

"We'll probably be able to hear each other if we shout," he said, mostly to reassure himself. "Just in case, if I tug three times, it means I want you to start pulling."

"And if *I* tug three times, it means you have to come out. Be careful."

He nodded in reply and ducked into the passage.

After only half a dozen steps, Raffa found that he could stand up straight. The ceiling wasn't entirely closed; there were cracks and gaps similar to those in the cave. These openings let in enough light to see by, although there wasn't much to look at, just limestone walls all around.

The narrow passage sloped gradually downward. Raffa was encouraged by this; it meant that he was getting closer to the point where Echo had entered the cliff face.

"All steady?" Kuma called, her words reaching him clearly.

"Steady," Raffa answered.

He continued walking forward. Once he had to clamber past a boulder that partially blocked his way. Then something brushed his face, and he let out a startled grunt. He stopped walking and looked around. What was it, a spiderweb?

The faintest of sounds . . . no, more like a ruffling of the air than a sound.

And something brushed past him again.

"Bats!" Raffa exclaimed.

The winged creatures flew past him in ones and twos, up the passage and then out through the openings overhead. It made sense: Sunfall was coming on, their prime hunting time.

As he watched, more and more bats joined the exodus. They were small creatures with large ears, just like Echo. Raffa kept trying to spot Echo, but he couldn't make out one tiny bat among the dozens now streaming past him.

"Echo! Echo, where are you?"

The bats continued to fly past, in greater numbers than he ever could have imagined. It was as if the entire cliff were hollow, its interior filled with bats.

Suddenly it was over, as unexpectedly as it had started. A few last bats fluttered past, and the passage was empty again.

Empty, and silent.

Raffa drew in a long breath. As he let it out, he felt a familiar *whump* on his chest.

"Ouch!" Echo said, as he missed the perch twig and dug his claws into the wool of Raffa's tunic.

Echo peered up at him, his dark eyes glowing with

the purple sheen borne by all the animals that had been treated with the scarlet vine from the Forest of Wonders.

"Raffa good?" Echo asked.

Raffa gave a shout of laughter. His relief on being reunited with Echo mounted even higher: Echo seemed his old self again!

"I'm fine, Echo," he said, trying to speak calmly. "What happened? Where did you go? You were sick, and now you seem so much better—"

Echo chittered, then fluttered off the perch and flew to the wall. "Echo go, Raffa come," he said.

He led Raffa down the passage for several more steps. It grew darker, as light from the cliff top faded. A faint odor curled through the air, slightly sulfurous but not unpleasant. It was warmer, too; Raffa was beginning to perspire under his tunic.

The passage hooked to the left, back to the right, and once more to the left. Then it seemed to end. But above a chest-high shelf of rock, there was a cleft just wide enough to slip into.

It took Raffa three tries to hoist himself onto the shelf. As he climbed through the cleft, Echo clicked sharply. Raffa stopped just in time, teetering on his tiptoes.

An enormous cavern opened out in front of him.

It looked to be at least twenty paces across. The ceiling arched high overhead, obscured by clouds of steam wafting through the air.

And there was no floor, for the cavern held an enormous hot spring.

Raffa had seen a hot spring before: There was one in the Forest of Wonders not too far from his home. But that one wasn't much bigger than a bucket. He hadn't even known that a hot spring could be this large, and he wondered if any human had laid eyes on the cavern before. Maybe he was the first person ever to see it!

Raffa groped through his rucksack for the lightstick. The rag on the end was soaked in an essence of phosphorescent fungi, invented by Raffa's mother, Salima. It produced a greenish light, not very strong, but certainly better than nothing.

The rock on which he stood curved out over the water. At its base, there was a narrow lip barely wide enough for his feet and only if he stood heel-to-toe. Cautiously he lowered himself onto the lip; he had to crouch to keep from hitting his head on the underside of the rock. Then he held the lightstick out as far as he could reach.

The dark surface of the water was in constant, gentle

motion. In a few places around the edge of the spring, bubbles chuckled and popped. Careful to keep his balance, he leaned forward and stuck a tentative finger into the water. It was pleasantly warm.

To his left, he saw a stream of bubbles. He sidled over, put his hand into the stream—and drew it out with a jerk. The water there was much hotter!

Raffa guessed that the spring was yet another legacy of the Great Quake. It was surely heated by magma that had made its way to the surface through fissures created during the Quake.

To Raffa's surprise, Echo alit on the ledge next to him. The bat almost never landed on the ground. His claws, so perfectly formed for grasping, were nearly useless on a flat surface.

"Beetle," Echo said happily. Waddling awkwardly, he began snapping at something on the ground, almost as if he were a bird.

Raffa brought the lightstick closer. In its dim glow, he could see small insects moving about.

"Echo no good, eat beetle, Echo good," the bat explained.

So it was these insects that had made Echo feel better!

Although some of the insects seemed to be scurrying

aimlessly—doubtless trying to elude Echo's probing snout—others were crawling with more purpose, in a ragged line toward the edge of the spring. Raffa followed them with his eyes and saw that their destination was a clump of plants.

Growing in the midst of one of the bubble-streams, the plants didn't have anything that looked like leaves. Instead they had a network of fine, hairlike stems, almost as if their root balls were above instead of below. Numerous insects were munching away at the stems.

In the greenish light, Raffa wasn't sure at first what color the plants were. Certainly they wouldn't be green themselves, for no sunlight reached the cavern. As he looked more closely, he saw that the stems were color-less, almost translucent.

Then the bubbles started belching loudly, as a spurt of hot gas pulsed into the spring from deep within the earth. Raffa stared in astonishment.

The plants had begun to glow. The tip of each tiny stem burned brightly with a clear white light. For the space of a single long breath, the cluster of plants shone like a ball of minuscule stars.

When the light vanished, the cavern was so dark that Raffa wondered if he had imagined the plants' illumination. He blinked a few times to clear his vision and his thoughts.

The fungi distilled for his lightstick emitted a pale green light that glowed steadily. Cracklefruits sparked when you crunched down hard on them, and some botanicals produced dull gleams when they were being ground in the mortar. But this was different: The plant's intense light was like nothing he had ever seen before.

Raffa frowned. That wasn't quite true. He *had* seen that kind of brilliance produced by a botanical: by the scarlet vine, whenever he pounded it into a paste.

He sat very still, thinking hard.

Every plant he knew of needed sunlight to survive. Even the fungi found in dark or shadowy places drew nourishment from rotting plant matter that had itself grown in the sun. This cavern plant was living entirely without sunlight. It seemed to be using the gases that percolated through the spring as a replacement for the sun's rays.

As if in confirmation, the water roiled more energetically, and the plants again flashed their dazzling display.

Raffa felt his heartbeat speeding up. It was beyond astonishing: Not even Uncle Ansel, with all his adventuring and exploring, had ever mentioned such a possibility!

Another thought struck him. True enough that the plant's mere existence was an amazement, but it was also highly likely that it possessed apothecary qualities. Echo had apparently cured himself by eating insects that fed on this plant.

His excitement mounting, Raffa began to gather part of the plant nearest him, automatically following the time-honored apothecary rules: Never take more than a quarter of the plant, and do as little damage as possible to that which remained. He worked with his hands underwater, teasing out the roots.

Another spurt of hot gas bubbled up, almost scalding him.

"Ouch!" he exclaimed as he jerked his hand out of the water.

"Ouch?" Echo repeated. "No ouch now. Ouch later. Eat beetle now."

Raffa laughed. When the bat was first learning to talk, he had flown to Raffa but missed the perch and grabbed skin instead. Raffa had said "Ouch!" and ever since, Echo had used the word to mean something like *"Landing!"*

"That's fine, Echo. Go ahead, keep eating."

Raffa finished his work on the plant and put it

carefully into his rucksack, then scanned the cavern. At least a dozen more clumps of the plant were spaced unevenly around the edge of the spring. He should try to harvest as much as he could. If the plant proved useful, there was no telling when he'd be able to return to the cavern to gather more.

Several craggy outcrops protruded from the cavern wall. Was there a way he could use them to reach the plants? If he could climb the wall, maybe he could hang from one of the crags. . . .

Raffa stood and retraced his steps partway up the passage, to the boulder he'd climbed past on his way down. He craned his head around it.

"Kuma!" he shouted. "I need the rope—leave go the end!"

"Are you sure?" Her voice was faint, but he could hear the words plainly.

"Yes, I'm fine. And Echo's fine, too! I'll tell you about it later."

"Well, if you're okay, then I'm going to take Twig down to the river—she's thirsty. I'll come back to check on you."

"Fine. I'll probably be a while, so take your time." He pulled on the rope and hauled in its loose end.

It did not take long for Raffa to realize that his plan wouldn't work. The cavern walls were slippery with condensation, and all the crags were well out of reach. He tried several times to throw a noose over the nearest one, but he didn't even come close. Disappointed, he stared across the cavern at the plants he would be unable to harvest.

There was one clump to his right that might just be within reach. Raffa propped the lightstick against the cavern wall. He squatted down on the lip of rock and extended his arm out as far as he could. His fingertips brushed the tops of the nearest stems.

If he could shift his weight, and stretch . . . just a little . . . bit . . . more—

SPLASH!

CHAPTER FIVE

F OR the second time that day, Raffa found himself
underwater.

At least this time it's warm, he thought as he kicked
his way to the surface. He had no idea how deep the
spring was; he knew only that he hadn't touched bottom
when he'd fallen in.

Raffa saw that he wouldn't be able to haul himself
from the water to the lip on which he had been standing. It was much too narrow, with the curved rock rising
behind it. He would have to find somewhere else to
climb out.

He swam a slow circuit around the edge of the

spring. Helpfully, the plants lit up at irregular intervals, enabling him to see for moments at a time.

There was no place suitable. Raffa swam around again, hoping that he had missed a spot in the dark. This time, he trailed one hand along the edge as he paddled.

No ledge anywhere.

He tried twice to boost himself onto the narrow lip from which he had fallen, but the rock curved out above it—exactly enough for him to bash his head on, which happened on his second attempt.

Let's not do that again, he thought ruefully as he treaded water.

Even though he knew it was probably futile, he tried yelling.

"Kuma!" he hollered.

Silence, except for the sound of bubbles popping.

"Kuma? *KUMA!*"

To his dismay, the water seemed to absorb the sound of his voice. He realized, too, that his shouts were likely blocked by the zigzag in the passage and probably by the boulder as well.

Echo seemed to sense his distress, for he chittered anxiously as he swooped nearby. At the sight of the little bat, Raffa slapped himself on the head. *How quake-brained could a person be?*

"Echo! Echo, will you fly out and find Kuma and tell her I need her help? She's down near the river."

He realized that it would be difficult for Kuma to pull him out of the water, but he was sure that together they could figure out a way.

He floated on his back, waiting. Whenever the plants lit up, he surveyed the cavern's walls and ceiling. He noticed that there was very little guano on the walls. Bats didn't roost in this cavern; the hot spring probably made it too warm for them.

It seemed a long time before Echo returned and alit on the cavern wall.

"Friend Kuma not river," the bat reported.

Not there? Then where could she be?

It was no use sending Echo to Garith. He wouldn't be able to hear Echo's words, nor read the bat's tiny lips. Besides, given the mood he'd been in lately, he would probably just ignore Echo.

Raffa felt a prickle of panic. He quashed it by forcing himself to think one thought at a time.

The water's warm.

I can float on my back if I get tired.

Sooner or later, Kuma will wonder what I'm about.

But would he be able to keep himself afloat that long? Raffa groaned, recalling his own words to her: *I'll probably be a while, so take your time.*

Twice more, he sent Echo on unsuccessful searches for Kuma.

Where is *she?* Raffa tried to smother his frustration, which had begun to border on anger. It wasn't Kuma's fault, and he knew that the anger was spurred by his growing fear.

At least he wasn't alone. Echo circled once overhead, then flew to a crag that jutted out over the cleft. As Raffa watched him, an idea came to him. He reached up and grabbed the rope from the ledge, uncoiled its full length, and held one end overhead.

"Echo! Can you come get the rope, please?"

The bat flew to him willingly. On the second try, Echo was able to grasp the end of the rope in his tiny claws. Still damp from having been in the river, the rope was heavy for the little bat. He flapped his wings hard to stay airborne.

"Echo, that crag where you just were—will you take the rope up there and drop the end over it?"

Echo struggled through the air and reached the crag. He opened his claws and the rope fell over the crag.

"Echo good!" Raffa cheered.

But the hardest part was still to come. Echo would have to take the end of the rope and circle the crag so the rope would be looped around it.

They tried dozens of times.

"No, not that way, Echo. *Down* first—go *under* and then back up . . ."

"That was good, Echo! Now can you do it again, but this time holding the rope?"

"Left—go left now! *Left*, I said!"

Echo finally squealed in frustration. "Left? What left? *WHAT LEFT?*"

Raffa floated on his back, panting. Of course Echo wouldn't know what *left* was. In the past Raffa had always used the sun's position—daybirth or sunpeak or sunfall—when he wanted to direct the bat's flight. Here in the cavern, there was no way of knowing where the sun was.

He looked at his fingertips, wrinkled and sodden. He had been in the water for a long time, and he could feel his body beginning to tire.

The water bubbled; the plants emitted their brilliant light. Overhead, Raffa saw the end of the rope dangling uselessly from the crag. It wasn't Echo's fault; what he'd already managed to do with the rope was heroic enough. The rest was just too complicated.

But they had to try again; Raffa had no other choice.

"Echo," he started to say.

"Echo go," the bat said.

"No, don't leave! Please, we have to try—"

"Echo go, Echo come."

The bat was gone before Raffa had a chance to speak again. Then the light from the plants vanished, and seemed to take most of his hope with it.

Still, he found that he couldn't give up. He tried putting his elbows on the lip of rock so he could rest, but they kept slipping off. With grim irony, it occurred to him that drowning in the Everwide might well have been preferable. The icy cold had numbed him into unconsciousness, which wouldn't happen here in the hot spring. A question he'd never asked himself before: Would he rather drown in cold water or warm? His thoughts were growing bleaker by the moment.

Think! he shouted at himself. *There must be another way. . . . THINK!*

But no plan or idea came to him. He alternated

between treading water and floating on his back. Each minute seemed longer than the last.

How long would he be able to keep this up? Could he stay afloat long enough for Kuma to worry and make her way through the passage to find him?

Click click chitter.

Echo was back!

"Echo!"

The bat landed on the crag, then squeaked out, "Raffa good?"

Raffa couldn't help laughing. He didn't know why he felt so joyful; there was nothing the bat could do to help. Maybe, he thought, maybe people just don't like to be alone when they're in trouble.

In the next glow of light from the plants, he saw to his surprise that Echo was not alone. At least half a dozen bats had flown into the cavern with him.

Several more bats arrived. Then more, and still more, and soon the cavern was filled with bats, flapping and squeaking and clicking in what seemed to be pure chaos.

But Raffa was wrong about that. It wasn't chaos. In the next few moments, he watched in puzzlement as a large group of bats flew to the crag to join Echo.

A second group, even bigger than the first, then landed on the crag. They folded their wings and hung upside down, crowding together. More and more followed, dozens, hundreds, until the entire crag was covered with layer upon layer of bats.

With a burst of utter astonishment, Raffa realized that the first layer of bats were now pinning the rope to the rock with their little claws, and all the other bats were keeping them in place!

He grabbed the rope and wrapped it around his chest several times until he had taken up almost all the slack. After tying it securely under his armpits, he took hold of it in both hands and gave it a tentative tug.

Miraculously, the rope held!

He tugged harder. The bats squealed in protest, but the rope remained firm.

Hand over hand, Raffa raised himself out of the water. Then he kicked his legs to start the rope swinging.

On the crag, the mass of bats shifted perilously. The cavern filled with their shrieks of distress. They were such small creatures. . . . There was no way they would be able to hang on long enough. . . .

One last swing: Using muscles he didn't know he had, Raffa thrust his feet over the top of the rock and into the cleft—just as he felt the rope give.

It whipped away from the crag, the bats scattered like autumn leaves in a tempest, and Raffa fell, his face bashing the edge of the rock.

Never had a split lip felt so good.

CHAPTER SIX

S Raffa sat up, he saw that most of the bats were leaving the cave. A few lingered on the crag near Echo; he could hear their squeaks and clicks.

How had Echo known how to save him? How had he summoned the other bats? Raffa shook his head in wonder. He'd have to ask Echo later.

He touched his lip; it was a little swollen, but the bleeding had already stopped. Taking deep breaths, he sat quietly until his pulse calmed. At last he stood and checked the rest of his body parts. His legs felt wobbly after all that time in the water. He had a scrape on his shin and a bruise on his side, but everything moved the way it was supposed to.

A good thing, because he had work to do.

He was, after all, an apothecary: Two near-drownings and one impossible rescue were shoved to the back of his mind by the excitement of discovering a new plant!

Raffa headed up the passage to the boulder. He tied the rope around it securely, then returned to the spring, muttering to himself: He should have thought of using the boulder in the first place. Why did good ideas so often get buried under the bad ones?

Now safely tethered, Raffa went back into the water and harvested portions of several more plants. By the time he finished, his rucksack was full. Finally satisfied, he used the rope to haul himself out and stood atop the rock, taking a last look at the wondrous cavern.

The plants glowed again. In their light, Raffa saw that Echo was still interacting with the other bats. He started to call out, but Echo's name lodged in his throat.

Raffa closed his mouth slowly. It was the first time he had seen Echo with other bats, and it looked . . .

Normal.

No, that's not quite the right word—

Natural. The way bats always were, except for Echo. Raffa heard Kuma's voice in his head: *The way they're supposed to be.*

Raffa stuck out his chin. "Echo!" he shouted. The cavern multiplied the sound of his shout, making it much louder. "Come on, we have to go."

To his relief, Echo flew to the perch at once. Raffa put the bat under his tunic. Then he climbed out of the passage and into the light.

It felt like he had been gone a long time.

When Raffa reached the cave, he found it empty, just as Echo had reported. "Kuma?" he called from the ledge outside.

He jumped a foot in the air when her head popped up from under the ledge, almost right in front of him.

"I found another cave," she said. "Not as high as this one. It's better, closer to the river."

Her voice, neither surprised nor concerned, reminded him that she had no way of knowing what had happened in the cavern. Then she looked at the water dripping from his clothes and pooling at his feet. "Why are you so wet again?" she asked.

"Go on back down. I'll follow you," he said. "Faults and fissures, do I have a story to tell!"

Roo and Twig seemed happy exploring the new cave, so Kuma left them there and met Raffa at the bottom of the cliff. Together they walked over to Garith, who sat up and rubbed his eyes, looking sullen.

Despite his excitement, Raffa reminded himself to talk slowly and keep his face toward Garith. "You'll—never—be-lieve—what—hap-pened! There's—a—huge—cavern—"

"For quake's sake!" Garith shouted. "How many times do I have to tell you? When you talk like that, it's *harder* for me to read your lips, not easier! I have to get used to people talking at normal speed—I've told you and told you, and you never listen!"

Raffa stood with his mouth gaping in surprise. He snapped it shut, then stammered, "I—I—"

He didn't know what to say. It was true that Garith had said this often, and equally true that Raffa had ignored it. But that was because it didn't make sense to him. He was only trying to help. Couldn't Garith see that?

Kuma glanced from one cousin to the other. She touched Garith's arm so he would look at her. "We're all tired," she said, her voice quiet but firm. "We need to eat and rest. Garith, would you gather some firewood?" She picked up a stick on the ground and handed it to him. "Raffa and I will fetch water and do some foraging."

Garith's face did not lose its petulant frown, but he nodded and got to his feet. Kuma took Raffa by the arm and steered him toward the river.

Now Raffa was annoyed as well as confused. He thought back to the winter months, when he had often returned from doing Garith's share of the chores to find him patching a basket or making snowshoes. He realized that it must have been Kuma who had assigned him those tasks; Garith wouldn't have known how to do them if she hadn't shown him. Raffa wished he could deal with Garith as well as Kuma did.

His scowl was interrupted by a cry of delight from Kuma.

"Raffa—cattails!"

He looked up and saw a large stand of cattails where the river ran through a stretch of swampy ground. There were plenty of shoots, as well as some mature spikes covered with yellow dust.

"Pollen!" Raffa exclaimed, his glumness lifting instantly.

It was early in the year for pollen, but the gorge was so sheltered that it was much warmer than the mountains. Cattail pollen could be used like flour. Dinner that night would be a special treat!

Kuma borrowed a square of linen from Raffa's ruck-sack and began collecting the pollen. While Raffa gathered shoots, he told her all about his perilous time in the cavern.

She stared at him, her eyes wide. "Oh, no," she said. "We climbed down and I let Twig drink, and we were coming back up when I found the other cave. So we stayed there for a while. I wanted them to get used to it. And Echo couldn't see me because I was inside it. I should never have left—"

"Maybe not," Raffa said, "but I was the one who said I'd be a while. We'll just have to watch out for each other better from now on."

Then he gave Echo a gentle pat. "Echo, how did you know to fetch all the other bats? What made you think of it?"

The little bat blinked. He seemed confused by the question.

"Raffa want rope stay," he said. "Echo one, rope not stay. Bats many, rope stay."

Kuma nudged him. "Yah, Raffa," she said. "What's the matter with you—it's as simple as that!"

And she laughed so hard that Raffa had to join in.

* * *

Garith had a fire going by the time they got back. Kuma added water to the cattail pollen to make a thick dough. She rolled the dough into a snake, divided it into three pieces, and wrapped each piece around a green stick of mountain ash. They roasted the dough spirals over the fire.

Raffa was so eager to sample his that he burned the roof of his mouth. The cattail bread was fire-blackened outside, heavy and pasty within. But after an entirely breadless winter, it tasted wonderful. He only wished they'd had salt to season the dough.

Garith said little during the meal. The trio finished eating and cleaning up, then put down leafy boughs for beds. As Raffa warmed his hands at the fire, Garith came and stood next to him.

"I'm leaving in the morning," he said. "I'm going back to Gilden."

"To Gilden?" Raffa frowned. "We can't—"

Garith held up his hand to stop him. "It's dark, with just the fire," he said. "It's hard for me to see your lips."

Raffa turned to face Garith directly. "We can't go to Gilden; we'd be arrested as soon as we got anywhere near the Commons." As a gesture for "arrested," he held his hands out, wrists together as if they were shackled.

"I saw you say 'we,'" Garith said. "Not we, just *me*.

I'm going on my own. It's got nothing to do with you."

I can't let him go alone, Raffa thought. Anything could happen. . . . What if he doesn't hear something that might hurt him?

He cleared his throat. "Garith, I don't think that's a good idea."

Garith stared at him for a moment. "I didn't ask what you think."

"Come on, Garith," Raffa said. He tried to lighten the mood by clasping his hands and shaking them in a mock plea. "When I get home and you're not with me, Mam won't even let me in the house."

No laugh. Not even a smile.

But Garith did look a little wistful at the mention of Salima. She was Garith's aunt, and she had always treated him as her own child.

Then he shook his head. "I have to see my da."

Raffa reached out and patted Garith's arm. "You will, Garith. Soon. I promise."

Garith shook off Raffa's hand and turned on him, his eyes blazing. "Are you—you—" he sputtered in anger. "There you go again, treating me like a baby!"

"No, that's not what I—"

Garith strode past, shouldering Raffa out of the way.

Raffa staggered back a step and caught himself. Fists clenched, he shouted at Garith's back.

"Don't you walk away from me like that!"

But, of course, Garith didn't hear him.

Raffa stamped his foot and started after Garith. Kuma caught his tunic sleeve and held it. "Let him go," she said quietly.

"Why are you always interfering?" Raffa snapped.

Kuma drew back with a scowl. "*Always?* That's not fair, and you know it."

She was right, but Raffa was too far gone in anger now. "Just stay out of it!" he shouted.

He saw the hurt in her eyes and immediately regretted his outburst. "Kuma—"

She too spun away, and went to sit with Roo and Twig beneath a nearby tree.

Raffa's anger dissolved into bewilderment. What had just happened? All he was trying to do was get them home safely, and neither Garith nor Kuma seemed to appreciate that. Was this what being a leader was like? Clearly, he wasn't very good at it. How did you get better? Was it just a matter of trying?

Maybe it's like apothecary, trying different combinations. Only instead of botanicals, combinations of words, and—and how I say things, and what I do.

Sober and thoughtful, he lay down on his makeshift pallet, reached for his rucksack, and pulled it under his head for a pillow. As if matching his mood, the rucksack was utterly uncomfortable. It was too high, being stuffed full of the cavern plant.

Raffa sat up in one abrupt motion.

The cavern plant.

He remembered the moment he had learned of Garith's deafness and the vow he'd made then and there: He had sworn to himself that he would try to invent an antidote, and that he would never give up trying.

His face flamed with shame. Months had passed during which he had done less than nothing toward that goal. There were reasons, of course, and they were good ones. In the Suddens, he had had very few botanicals, almost no equipment, and, most important of all, no time. The struggle for food and warmth had taken up nearly every minute of every day.

But he hadn't even *tried*. No, it was worse than that: He had barely given it a thought! Garith had every reason to be angry at him; indeed, Raffa was angry at himself. It was clear to him now that he hadn't *wanted* to think of it.

Because he was fully aware that deafness had never been cured by an infusion, and he was afraid of failing.

He lay down again, his thoughts churning. *What if . . . what if I could pretend—even for a little while—that there's a cure out there and I just have to find it?*

To his surprise, it wasn't hard to pretend. Instead of thinking about Garith's deafness, he began considering combinations of botanicals, especially the mysterious cavern plant. Like the scarlet vine, the cavern plant might well have healing and curing properties. Was it possible . . . Could he use the plant to create a cure for Garith's deafness?

The first image that came to his mind was, of all things, a cork. A cork being inserted into the bung of a barrel to stop liquid from flowing out. Raffa lay very still and let his thoughts float freely, rather than forcing them in any particular direction. And in a few moments, the barrel had transformed into the vague outlines of a human face—with the cork stuck up one nostril!

Congestion! Raffa twitched with excitement, but then he made himself relax again.

When people's noses are congested, their ears sometimes get stopped up, too. The infusion for that . . . appletip vinegar combined with mint leaf and marjo oil.

I'll make that combination—in all different strengths and add the cavern plant— No, first I have to make a bunch of poultices, to make sure it's safe. . . .

Experimenting with botanicals was Raffa's favorite part of apothecary work. After a day of too much peril and confusion, it was both exciting and soothing to think on. He fell asleep with his mind full of leaves, petals, roots, and stems, all swirling in patterns and colors both beautiful and strange.

He began to dream almost immediately. The colorful swirls were receding, moving away from him. *No, no—don't go!* He reached for them, but whenever his hand closed around one, it faded into grayness. He wanted them so badly! Every muscle and nerve in his body strained toward them, wishing, aching, yearning. . . .

Raffa opened his eyes. Wide awake, he understood at once what his dream meant.

Yearnings.

Yearnings were desires that could not be treated by apothecary. Often they were foolish wishes: great wealth, the ability to fly, control over another person. Raffa's parents, especially his father, Mohan, worked hard to make sure that their patients understood the capabilities and limitations of apothecary.

But there were other kinds of yearnings. Salima had once spoken about the desperate need to create cures for illnesses considered incurable. Those sorts of yearnings were worthy of an apothecary's attention. The problem was that no one knew which diseases and conditions might one day prove treatable.

Raffa's dream was telling him what he already knew, as dreams so often did: Hard work and time and creativity would not make success a certainty. Even if he vanquished his fear of failure, it was still a very real possibility. A thousand experiments might not produce a cure for Garith.

Raffa pressed his lips together and scowled in determination.

It didn't matter. He still had to try.

When he woke the next morning, it was just past daybirth, still shadowy in the gorge. He rubbed his eyes clear of sleep-blur, then turned to look beyond the fire toward the other pallets.

He rose to his knees, frowning.

Kuma was asleep across from him. But the third pile of boughs was empty.

Garith was gone.

CHAPTER SEVEN

RAFFA leapt to his feet. He circled the campsite in a panic, searching wildly for signs of Garith's trail, before his common sense asserted itself.

They were close to the Southern Woodlands now. Garith would take the straightest trail north to get to Gilden. And the easiest way to do that was to follow the river.

Kuma was still asleep. Roo had spent the night in a hollow at the base of a big neverbare, with Twig curled up next to her.

"Echo!" Raffa called. "Echo, where are you? I need you!"

The bark of the tree's trunk flickered with movement. Echo had been perched several feet above Roo's head. He flew to the necklace, landing with his customary "Ouch."

"Echo, would you please fly north—that way, away from sunpeak—and tell me if you see Garith anywhere?"

Kuma had woken and was now standing beside him.

"No," she said. "You won't find him. He left hours ago."

Raffa stared at her. "You saw him leave? You—you knew, and you let him go?"

She looked back at him steadily. "Perfect moon was two nights ago, so there was plenty of light. He'll follow the river, and it will join up with the road. He won't get lost."

"But he can't hear! What if— Something terrible might happen to him—"

"Roo and I walked him out of the gorge. He'll get to the Southern Woodlands soon. Nothing there can hurt him."

Kuma reached out her hand, almost but not quite touching him. "Raffa, he couldn't leave things as they are with his father. He had to go back, no matter . . .

no matter what he finds there. And he had to go on his own, without our help. If he doesn't do it now, he might be afraid forever." A pause. "No one likes feeling helpless. Or useless."

Her words triggered a memory so strong that Raffa almost winced. At home, his father, Mohan, had for years given him only menial apothecary tasks to do. Raffa had hated doing work that he considered of little value.

Was that how he had made Garith feel? All the long winter, when Raffa had toiled so hard doing Garith's share of the work, he thought he was taking care of his poor deaf cousin. Well, Garith was deaf sure enough, but maybe Raffa's pity was the last thing he'd needed.

Kuma folded her arms and held her elbows, almost as if she were hugging herself. "He made me realize that I have to go home, too."

Raffa's eyes widened in surprise. Kuma had been raised by her aunt and uncle, who had a large family of their own; she had once told Raffa that they never missed her when she stayed for days at a time with Roo in the Forest of Wonders.

"I don't suppose they're worried," she said slowly, answering his unvoiced question. "But they were kind enough to take me in, and I don't have any other family, except for Roo, and I owe it to them to let them know that—that I'm still drawing breath."

Raffa had never fully realized before how fortunate he was when it came to family. Garith, heading for Gilden, with no idea how his father would react. Kuma, not knowing if her family had even missed her all this time. Whatever doubts and worries Raffa had, they did not include the welcome he would receive from his parents: Their reunion would overflow with relief and joy and love.

"Echo's better. He doesn't need my parents' help," Raffa said slowly. "But I'm still going home, because— because home is where you go when you don't know what else to do."

It was as if Echo's illness had half-blinded Raffa to nearly everything else. Now he could see that the bat's health had been only one of many reasons for getting home—and probably the least important, if he were being honest.

Garith's depression. The Chancellor's schemes. Uncle Ansel's role in those schemes, and his use of apothecary. The trapped animals . . . Raffa could only hope that winter had played its usual part in slowing the pace of life, including, especially, the Chancellor's plot. He had to reach his parents and tell them everything. They would figure out what to do.

Kuma's voice interrupted his thoughts. "Still friends?" she asked.

He felt a flicker of shame that she even had to ask.

"Of course," he said firmly, and meant it.

While Raffa cleaned up the campsite, Kuma went to the river and collected several handfuls of large pebbles. She left the pebbles in random piles at the base of the cliff. With their smooth round and oval shapes, they looked quite different from the chips and shards of limestone that had fallen from the cliff face. But anyone who didn't know that the river rocks were there would be highly unlikely to notice them.

Then Kuma and Roo climbed to a ledge on the cliff halfway between the floor of the gorge and the chosen cave, where there were several saplings crowded together. At Kuma's request, Roo used her tremendous strength to pull and push one of the small trees until it was partially uprooted. It was now leaning against the cliff, its root ball half exposed.

"How does that look?" Kuma called down.

Raffa tipped his head back. The tree looked like it could have been pushed over in a bad storm.

Kuma was marking the location of the cave so she could find it again when she returned to the gorge to visit Roo. She was using the tree and the pebbles as signposts; they looked natural enough not to give away the site to anyone else.

Twig had followed her bear-mother up the cliff and was now pawing at the tree's root ball. "Bugs!" she said. "Bugs bugs bugs!" She snorted and chuffed joyfully.

The root ball harbored a whole universe of insects and grubs. Twig's delight made it clear that they were especially scrumptious. Roo plunked herself down next to Twig and began eating, too.

With a sigh of resignation, Raffa climbed the cliff to join the group. After watching the bear and raccoon eat for a few minutes, Kuma crouched beside Roo and stroked the bear's haunch.

"I don't know when I'll be back, Roo," she said. "Like in the Forest, remember? Whenever I come, we'll find each other."

Her voice started to wobble. Raffa bent down and rubbed Twig's back gently. The little raccoon looked up at the two humans. She chirred and stretched her front paws out toward them; in each, she held a nice fat grub.

"Grrr-rum!" Twig squeaked. Raffa wouldn't have thought it possible to squeak a growl, but Twig somehow managed it. "Eat, eat, grrr-rum!"

"Oh!" Kuma said. "She wants to share with us—how sweet!"

Raffa looked at the grubs wriggling in Twig's grasp. "Adorable," he said, then waved his hand in a gesture of generosity. "You can have mine."

So there were tears upon laughter as Raffa and Kuma climbed back down the cliff, leaving Roo and Twig behind.

With nearly every step he took through the gorge, Raffa thought of Garith, who would have traveled the same route, not diverging until beyond the next stretch of forest, when he would head for the ferry landing. Raffa searched for signs of his cousin's journeying—a footprint in soft ground, a broken twig on a shrub . . .

Nothing. Raffa knew it was foolishness, but he couldn't stop wishing for some way of knowing that Garith was safe.

Kuma, too, was preoccupied, and finally spoke up. "Do you think Roo is still in danger?" she asked. "It's been months, you know. Maybe they've given up on the idea. . . ."

Raffa did not reply, because he knew she wouldn't want to hear what he was thinking. He had only to recall the vicious determination in Chancellor Leeds's voice during their escape: There was no doubt in his mind that she would be searching for Roo again, now that the ice and snow were nearly gone. Was the cave in the remote gorge a safe enough hiding place?

He sought to reassure Kuma. "You know, Twig is like a cub to Roo," he said.

That brought a smile to her face, but a tentative one.

"It's not just, you know, sweet and cute and all that," he continued. "It means she'll do anything to keep Twig from harm. They'll both be that much safer."

"That's solid truth," she said, her expression brightening. "I wouldn't want to be Jayney or Trubb trying to get close to Roo while she's protecting Twig!"

Then she tapped Raffa's arm. "Would it be okay if—" She paused. "I mean, I'll understand if you say no—"

"Er, can I find out what I'd be saying no to?" he teased with a smile.

"Could I wear that for a little while?" She nodded at his neckline.

Raffa understood at once. Missing Roo, Kuma wanted to wear the perch necklace, where Echo was roosting, fast asleep. He took it off and handed it to her. She looked at him gratefully.

Echo emitted two clicks, his sleep disturbed by the movement of the perch. He opened his eyes groggily.

Kuma held the bat close and studied him for a moment.

"Raffa?" she said. "Look at his eyes."

Raffa glanced at the bat's small face. Echo blinked a few times, then went back to sleep.

"What about them?" Raffa asked, puzzled.

"Do they look any different to you?"

"Different how?"

"I—I—I'm not sure. Darker, maybe? I just thought—"

Darker? Raffa felt a twinge of unease.

When he first met Echo, the bat's eyes had been black. After being treated with the scarlet vine, his eyes had taken on a striking purple sheen. Twig had it, too—as did all the other animals in Gilden that had been given the vine infusion.

If Echo's eyes were turning dark again, could it mean that the effects of the vine infusion were wearing off? And if they did wear off, would Echo stop talking?

Would he want to return to the wild, to live with other bats again?

"I don't see any difference," Raffa declared. His voice sounded more belligerent than he had meant it to, so he added, "I'll check again later, when he's properly awake."

But he had no real intention of doing so. If there was any chance that Echo might leave him, he didn't want to know.

Raffa mapped the rest of their journey in his head. Southern Woodlands, Kuma's settlement, then the Eastern Woodlands. And, finally, home. Three days' walk if they made good time. The closer he got, the keener his longing to see his parents.

The woodlands lacked the mysterious and magical plants found in the Forest of Wonders; still, Raffa had always thought of them as untamed wilderness. Now as he and Kuma hiked its trails, he saw traces of human activity everywhere.

The trails themselves, of course. Clearings where trees had been cut for firewood. A stunning pink expanse of spring beauty blossoms, with swathes missing because their roots had been dug up for food. Raffa realized that the woodlands were hardly wilderness at all compared to the desolate reaches of the Suddens.

Toward sunpeak they crossed a small stream that branched off from the Everwide.

"Lunch?" Kuma suggested. "We can wash and drink here."

Raffa nodded. "But not for long," he said. "We should try to get out of these woods before dark."

They ate the last of the cattail-pollen bread and drank from the stream. After their meager lunch, they began walking again, and reached the edge of the woodlands by sunfall.

The leftovers of winter's chill tinged the air. Raffa wore his hood pulled up. He said little as they walked; Kuma spoke even less. She slowed her pace as the tree growth gave way to brush and meadow, and the trail broadened into a path.

"The settlement starts after that bend," she said quietly.

They exchanged glances, and Raffa could see his own thoughts in Kuma's expression.

Would guards be awaiting them?

PART II

CHAPTER EIGHT

A SETTLEMENT as small as Kuma's would not have its own guard station. But the Chancellor could have ordered guards posted there, as well as at the pother settlement where Raffa's family lived, which was what Raffa suspected she had done. The Chancellor had struck him as someone who did not give up easily, and who was accustomed to getting her way, no matter what it took.

Raffa pulled out the perch necklace. Echo was just stirring.

"Skeeto," Echo said. "Skeeto skeeto skeeto."

"Yes, Echo, I know it's your hunting time, but I need

to talk to you. We're going to be with other people again soon. Remember the way it was in Gilden? You mustn't talk unless we're alone."

"Don't talk," Echo said. "Talk Raffa good."

"Echo good," Raffa said.

Echo swayed a little on the perch. "Talk Kuma friend?" he said, which made Kuma smile.

"Yes, you can talk to her, too. But not when other people are around." Raffa had long harbored the fear that Echo might be kidnapped by someone who thought to profit from the bat's amazing ability to speak. He had trusted very few people with this secret.

"And before you go hunting, would you do me a favor? I need you to fly ahead down the path a little and tell me if anyone is there."

Echo flew off and returned only moments later.

"Cow big. Cow little. No human." He flapped away again almost before he had finished speaking.

Raffa and Kuma grinned. They rounded the bend, and sure enough, a cow and a calf came into view. They were pastured in a field flanked by a beech copse.

"We should still be careful," Kuma said. "There's a back way to the house. I'll go, and if it's all clear, I'll come fetch you."

She turned off the path into the brush. Raffa watched until she disappeared behind a hedgerow. He found a large rock nearby and sat down to wait.

Kuma was gone long enough for Raffa to grow restless. First he drank from his waterskin. Then he spent some time tightening the knots that joined the sections of his rope.

As he retied the last knot, a flock of starlings in the beech copse rose into the air as a single skein. Raffa's head jerked up; he was instantly on the alert. Something had disturbed the birds.

In the next moment, he heard hoofbeats. An unfamiliar voice shouted his name.

"Hoy, Santana! Raffa Santana!"

For an instant, Raffa's whole body was paralyzed with shock and fear. Then sheer instinct took over, and he quickly turned his head *away* from the voice, in the other direction. With that small motion, a desperate plan came to him.

He shaded his eyes with one hand and peered into the distance for a moment, as if searching for someone; at the same time, he pulled his hood farther forward. Only then did he look back to see a guard on a horse, stopped in the middle of the path a dozen paces away.

Raffa jumped to his feet, his mouth so dry that he had to force out the words. "Were you talking to me, Senior?"

The guard, with no insignia on his uniform, was *not* a senior, but using the title of respect couldn't hurt. Likewise, Raffa kept his head lowered as if in subservience, hoping that the guard wouldn't be able to see his face clearly.

"Quake-brain," the guard said with a scowl. "If your name's not Raffa Santana, then it ought to be clear upon crystal that I'm *not* talking to you."

"Sorry, Senior, very sorry . . ." Raffa ducked his head even lower.

"What's your name, boy?"

Raffa should have been ready for this question, and indeed he had expected it. But it seemed like every name he had ever known flew out of his head at that moment, and he blurted out the only one left.

"Cinders. Cinders Cat—er—Cattergood."

He had to suppress a giggle of pure nervousness. Cinders was the name of a cat that had once lived with his family.

The guard didn't even seem to hear him. "Looking for a boy name of Raffa Santana," he said. "He's better than twelve years old, so a good bit older than you. You see him, tell one of the settlement seniors, hear?"

"Yes, Senior."

Despite being in a state of near panic, Raffa found that he had to swallow a bubble of indignation. He had long resented the fact that he looked so much younger than his age; it was never easy to hear, even when it was saving his skin.

The guard pulled at the reins, turned the horse around, and galloped away.

Raffa's legs wobbled beneath him, and he sat down on the rock so hard that he bruised his rear end. But there was no time for satisfaction that his ruse had worked.

Guards *were* looking for him. Here, in Kuma's settlement, and surely at his own home as well. And if they were after him, they would be looking for her, too. Was she already in their grasp? Was that why she hadn't yet returned?

Raffa grabbed his rucksack and started running through the brush, in the direction Kuma had taken. At the hedgerow he stopped, panting hard, and peered through the bushes.

On the other side lay two fallow fields. Beyond them, he could just make out a small farmhouse. Earlier, Kuma had described the communal settlement: a dozen houses in a rough semicircle, facing a large common area that contained the farm buildings. Three barns and a stable; coops, folds, and pens for various animals; and several storage sheds. There was a big vegetable garden as well. The families worked the surrounding fields and pastures together, sharing both the labor and the harvest.

Raffa crept around the edge of the fields, keeping to the hedgerow. Closer now, he saw the back dooryard of the house. A large water barrel stood near the door. As Raffa studied the house, a slight movement caught his eye.

Kuma was hiding behind the water barrel. She was leaning toward the door, obviously eavesdropping.

Raffa looked around quickly, then scurried across the yard. Kuma whirled around at the sound of his footfalls. She glared at him and put a finger to her lips as he joined her behind the barrel.

Inside the house, a man was speaking, his voice loud with outrage.

"You've been watching our house for weeks, and there's been less than no sign of her! Why won't you believe us?"

My uncle, Kuma mouthed.

"We want to know where she is as much as you do!"

A woman's voice. "No, no—far more! All these years and she's never once given us a sliver of trouble. For her to disappear like this, for so long—something must be terribly wrong, and you won't tell us why you're looking for her!"

Her voice caught on a sob. Raffa tilted his head, glancing at Kuma in puzzlement. That was surely her aunt speaking, and she didn't sound at all like someone who didn't care. Kuma looked away from him, her lips pressed together.

"We've been over this before, more times than I can count." A different man's voice. "Those are my orders— to watch the house, and bring the girl in if she comes here. The reason why is of no concern to me. We're leaving, but we'll be back. If you hear from your niece and don't report it to the Commons, you'll regret it more than you can imagine."

After those ominous words, a door slammed. Raffa scooted around to the side of the house, where he could see the path that led to the road. The man leaving the house wore a guard's uniform. He mounted his horse and joined three other guards, including the one who had queried Raffa. All four trotted away on the road toward the ferry landing.

Kuma pointed toward the nearest part of the hedge-row. She and Raffa ducked behind it.

"They were guarding the house when I first got here," Kuma whispered. "That's why I was taking so long—I had to wait to see what they'd do. Finally the one at the back went into the house, just before you came, and said they were leaving. You heard most of the rest."

If the guards had been here ever since their escape from Gilden, why were they leaving now? Raffa pondered, frowning. It was no longer winter, but that couldn't be the reason. What else was different? What else had changed?

Garith.

Raffa stared at Kuma. "Garith must have reached Gilden," he said slowly, "and—and for some reason, that's made a difference, and they've called the guards away."

Two possibilities occurred to him, almost at the same moment. Garith could have deliberately misled the Chancellor. He might have said that Kuma and Raffa were hiding Roo in the Forest of Wonders, with the result that the guards had been ordered to search for them there.

Or maybe . . .

Raffa glanced away from Kuma. He didn't want her to read the worry in his eyes over the second option: Garith could have told the truth about Roo's whereabouts.

But even if that's so, there's nothing I can do about it right now. Raffa turned his thoughts to what he *could* do. He scanned the sky quickly. No sign of Echo, but as long as Raffa stayed in the area, the bat would find him.

"Come on," Raffa said, as he rose out of his crouch.

Kuma tugged at his sleeve in alarm. "Get down! Someone might see you!"

"We're going to see your aunt and uncle."

"Raffa, no!" Her eyes grew wide with alarm. "If they know I'm here, it could get them into terrible trouble! And us, too!"

"Kuma." He squatted down so he could look straight at her. "The guards are gone now. This might be our only chance. They're your family. You thought maybe they didn't care about you? I know what I heard just now. It's worth a whole quake of trouble for you to see them again."

He saw her eyes fill with tears. "You really think so?" she said, her voice barely audible.

"No, I don't think so," Raffa replied. "I *know* so."

He took her by the hand, and they walked toward the house.

Raffa was more than right. He saw Aunt Haddie, who was wearing a blue headcloth, step out the back door, her face dark like Kuma's, with the same high cheekbones. Her mouth fell open and her eyes widened when she caught a glimpse of her niece. She quickly raised her hand and indicated that Kuma and Raffa should stay where they were, hidden again behind the water barrel.

Then she disappeared inside, and immediately Raffa could hear sounds of urgent activity. It seemed that Kuma's aunt and uncle had had a plan in place for her return.

There was a jumble of voices for several moments, and then the door slammed again. Raffa heard Haddie's footfalls inside, quick despite the generous girth of her body.

Then she reappeared at the door and pulled them both inside.

"The loft," she said. "Kuma, if they come back—the roof. You know."

Kuma nodded. She and Raffa scrambled up the ladder into the loft. Raffa listened to the sounds of Haddie busy below, all the while straining his ears for hoofbeats.

It seemed like a long time before he heard the door open, then the uncle's voice.

"The guards—they're well and truly gone."

Raffa and Kuma were sitting under the trapdoor to the roof, ready to climb out at the first sign of the guards' returning. Now they moved to peek over the edge of the loft floor into the room below.

Kuma's aunt and uncle stood in the unsteady light from the fireplace. All the shutters were closed.

"Come!" Aunt Haddie said. "Come here to me before I take another breath!"

When Kuma stepped off the ladder, Haddie hugged her so hard that she started coughing. Uncle Elson laughed and embraced Kuma, too. Then she introduced them to Raffa.

Elson held up his hand so Raffa could match palms with him. He was not a tall man, but still gave an impression of strength, with a sturdy neck and powerful shoulders. He wore his black kinked hair short and neat, and there was a plait in his beard.

"Oh, Kuma," Haddie said in a choked voice. "Did we not pay you enough mind? We were always grateful that you asked so little of us, but we never meant—"

"No, Aunt Haddie, please! It's not like that at all. I *couldn't* come home. I'll explain everything—but where are—"

"They're with people we trust," Elson answered.

Raffa noticed how Kuma and her aunt and uncle finished each other's sentences. He had done the same with his own family, and suddenly felt a surge of home-sickness.

"The Abduls have the older ones, and Missum Yuli took the babies," Elson went on. He turned to Raffa. "Our children—the oldest is only nine. They're not to know that Kuma is here. They might let something slip."

Raffa swallowed. "What about your neighbors?" he asked. "Will they . . . give us away?"

Elson shook his head. "Not Kuma," he said. "And we'll spread the word that you're with her."

"No more talk for now," Haddie said. "You both need a wash and a hot meal."

She had prepared huge basins of steaming hot water, one in each of the two smaller chambers flanking the main room. Raffa stripped off his clothes and sat down in the basin. The heat from the water soaked into his bones. He couldn't remember ever enjoying a wash as much as this one.

Haddie had left worn but clean clothes for him, a tunic and trousers and some underclothes. He did his best to ignore the realization that the garments, which fit him quite well, must have belonged to Kuma's nine-year-old cousin. After he dressed, he went back into the other room, where Kuma was just sitting down at the table. Bowls of hot corn mush awaited them.

Kuma tasted her mush. "You made this," she said immediately, looking up at her uncle. He nodded with a grin.

"Uncle Elson makes mush with honey and a little salt," she explained to Raffa. "Aunt Haddie makes it with butter."

"Bit of butter, much the better," Haddie said.

"No, mine's the better. Isn't that right, Kuma?" Elson teased in turn.

"I like them both," she said tactfully. Her next words were mumbled so softly that Raffa could barely hear them. "I've missed them both."

Raffa and Kuma ate heartily and scraped up every bite of mush. Haddie poured mugs of tea and handed them round to Elson and Raffa, but held the third mug in her hand and stared at Kuma, her mouth a straight line.

"Well, then!" she said, her eyes fierce. "You're warm and fed now, so suppose you tell me what gives you the right to leave us worried for—for months! A whole winter, Kuma, of not knowing if you—you—" Her hand began to tremble; she set the cup down so hard that tea sloshed out. "Tremors, now look what I've done!"

Kuma's eyes had grown wide at her aunt's display of emotion. Then she dropped her gaze to the tabletop for a long moment.

"I'm sorry, Aunt," she whispered. She looked first at Haddie and then at Elson; when she spoke again, her voice was a little louder, but thick with unshed tears. "Truly I am. And I'll tell the children sorry, too, when I see them."

"Oh, you're sorry, is it?" Haddie was wiping up the spill with a rag, scrubbing so hard that the table rocked. "I'm afraid that won't do, my dear. I know you're not one for talking, but it's going to take a good few more words than that to set things straight with us!"

Raffa saw Kuma swallow. She tried twice to speak, but nothing came out of her mouth. Finally she gazed pleadingly at Raffa.

"You start," she said.

* * *

The four of them talked long into the night. Raffa and Kuma took turns in the telling; Elson and Haddie asked questions, wondered, marveled.

There was so much to say. Echo and the scarlet vine. Roo and the baby raccoons. Garith, Ansel, Trixin, the Chancellor. The shed compound, the animals, the escape. The winter in the Suddens, the journey here. Raffa did not reveal Echo's speaking ability; still, he had never talked so much in his whole life, and he was sure that the same was even truer for Kuma.

When at last they finished, the silence around the table lasted a long time.

Elson sighed so deeply, it was more like a groan. "Either it's the truth or they're mistaken," he said.

Kuma glared at her uncle, her fists clenched. "You don't believe us?" she demanded.

Elson looked at her steadily. "I said mistaken, not lying. No one would invent such a tale. The question I keep asking myself is, Could there be a reasonable explanation?"

"Please," Raffa said. "I thought the same myself. For the longest time. Because of my uncle. I didn't want to think that he . . . But even if there *is* an explanation, what they're doing to the animals is bad upon worse."

"Surely you can see that!" Kuma pleaded.

"I do," Haddie said.

"I do as well." Elson leaned forward, his hands clasped on the tabletop. "I wonder, though—"

"You'll keep your wonder to yourself for the moment," Haddie cut in. "These two are for bed now and now."

She stood and moved behind the bench where Kuma was seated. Then she put her hands on Kuma's shoulders and gave the girl a shake that finished as a hug. "You're not forgiven," she said, "but at least I'm beginning to understand. Give me a bit longer, and I might get around to forgiveness."

Kuma turned and wrapped her arms around her aunt. Elson joined in to hug them both, and Raffa decided it would be a good moment to leave them alone.

On his way back from using the outhouse, he searched briefly for Echo. But the bat was still hunting somewhere; he would return in his own time.

Tiredness flooding through him, Raffa staggered to a pallet on the floor near the fire. His eyes closed even before he lay down.

He didn't know how long he slept before he began dreaming. In his dream, a dog was barking. Then another, and still another—sharp, frantic barks that went on and on. Raffa scowled in his sleep. He was so tired. . . . The dream-dogs were so loud. . . .

"Raffa! Raffa, wake up!"

Kuma was shaking his shoulder. Raffa opened his eyes. His whole brain felt bleary. The noisy barking continued, even shriller than before. Was he awake, or still dreaming?

"Outside!" Kuma shrieked. "Hurry!"

CHAPTER NINE

R AFFA ran to the door, his shoes unlaced. He
looked around in utter confusion.

It was the darkest part of the night. Clouds shielded
the moon. People were running everywhere, many carrying torches. Others held pitchforks or rakes or shovels.
The torchlight threw shadows that leapt and jerked constantly, adding to the chaos of noise and motion: people
shouting, dogs barking, chickens squawking, sheep
bawling.

Kuma had dashed away and now came running
toward him, holding two torches.

"Foxes!" she gasped out as she handed him a torch.

"Everywhere—they're after the sheep!"

"Torches! To the sheepfold, quickly!" Elson shouted, his deep, full voice cutting through the din.

Raffa followed Kuma as other torches ahead of them bobbed crazily in the darkness. At the sheepfold, people were forming a line circling the fence.

"All the way around!" Elson thundered. "Space yourselves—they could get in anywhere!"

Foxes appeared out of the darkness. They jumped and lunged, snapping their jaws, trying to get to the sheep. Inside the fence, the sheep screamed and stampeded in terror.

Raffa heard astonishment in the voices around him.

"What in the name of the Quake?"

"Foxes don't hunt in packs!"

"Where did they all come from?"

Again and again, Raffa thrust out his torch, waving it and yelling as fox after fox leapt toward him. The darkness and the flames, the people and foxes and sheep—it felt like a nightmare, and he wished fervently that he were still asleep.

Then a shout of panic: "They've broken through!"

The line of torches wavered as someone turned to climb the fence. Raffa watched in horror as at least half a dozen foxes streamed through the gap.

"Shepherds into the fold!" Elson shouted. "Everyone else, stand steady! Keep the line firm!"

Three people—whom Raffa could make out only by their torches—hopped the fence and began chasing the foxes inside the fold. The foxes stayed low to the ground; they were all but impossible to see among the panicked sheep.

Swinging his torch around, Raffa saw a blur of rust streak by, with white feathers flying everywhere.

"The chickens!" he screamed. "They're getting the chickens!"

The line of torches at the sheepfold shifted and stretched out as the people nearest the henhouse ran off, including Raffa and Kuma.

There are too many of them and not enough of us, Raffa thought.

The henhouse was easier to defend than the sheepfold. While Raffa and Kuma joined those keeping foxes away from the entrance, Haddie and three other people went inside. They chased out two foxes, but each fox carried off a chicken.

Raffa soon realized that he was no longer seeing purely by torchlight. The sky had shaded from black to dull gray. As he glanced up, he saw in the distance a small cloud much darker than the rest.

A chill shook him, and his body realized what it was before his mind did.

He had seen a cloud like that before.

"CROWS!" Raffa screamed. "Our eyes! We have to protect them!" The memory of the crows attacking him and Kuma during their escape from Gilden made fear boil up inside him. "Everyone, listen!"

But in the turmoil, no one seemed to hear. He had to find Elson; somehow the farmsteaders were attuned to his sonorous voice. Raffa ran back toward the sheepfold and saw Elson's silhouette against the wavering torchlight.

Elson listened to his urgent warning. For the first time, his staunchness wavered.

"What are we to do? We can't stop fighting the foxes, and we can't do it with our eyes covered!"

Before Raffa could answer, he was calling out again.

"Ears, everyone! There's a flock of crows approaching. If they get near you, duck and cover your eyes! You hear, give a hoy and pass the word along!"

A chorus of *Hoy*s sounded.

Elson's strategy was a sensible one, but Raffa's dread

deepened. He could not have expressed how terrifying the crows' assault had been. It took all his resolve not to throw himself on the ground that very moment, with his head buried in his arms.

The dark cloud drew closer. Raffa kept looking at it as he ran back toward the henhouse. The chickens were shrieking, and the din was brain-shaking. Then he saw to his horror that the foxes had been joined by stoats. Quicker and more agile than the foxes, the stoats seemed unfazed by the torches; they danced and dodged and did not retreat.

One more glance at the sky: The crows were nearly overhead. Raffa could wait no longer. "Everyone, cover your eyes!" he yelled.

He crouched down and buried his face in the crook of one arm while holding his torch up with the other. Maybe the fire would keep the crows away. . . .

He risked a quick peek to see that several other people had followed his example. Their eyes were protected— but at dreadful cost. The stoats now had unimpeded access to the henhouse.

Raffa lowered his face again and waited for the painful strike of a crow's beak. Several agonizing moments passed.

Nothing.

No sound of *craw* or flap of wings.

Puzzled, he lifted his head and saw that the crows were circling not over the henhouse or the sheepfold but above the storage sheds—where there were no people. Several at a time, they dropped down and flapped under the eaves.

"Kuma!" he shouted. "What's in those sheds?"

"Grain!" she shouted back. "Mostly wheat, some corn and oats—"

She looked as baffled as he felt. Were the crows eating the grain? There weren't enough of them to make a serious dent in the stores. The stoats and foxes were a far greater problem.

With one last look at the crows, they turned back to the henhouse.

Suddenly it was over.

The crows flew off. The stoats and foxes ran away from the settlement, vanishing as quickly as they had arrived.

In the thin light of daybirth, the farmsteaders gathered around the big barn. The toll was sobering. Four sheep were dead, another two badly mauled. Three chickens had been carried off. Worse still, more than thirty had been killed with a single bite to the head: the work of the stoats. Dozens of eggs had been smashed.

The younger children, including Kuma's cousins, were kept away from the grisly scene. A few of the adults took them on a morning walk away from the settlement. The other steaders worked with quiet diligence. Some tended the wounded animals; others butchered the dead sheep. Several teens went into the henhouse to sort the smashed eggs from those that were still whole.

Haddie led Raffa to Missum Yuli's home, where there was a small stock of botanica. Although the settlement did not have its own apothecary, Missum Yuli knew a little of healing. The city folk in Gilden were often mystified by or even a little afraid of apothecaries, but in the countryside, people were familiar with plant life and had great respect for the art of working with botanicals.

"This is Raffa," Haddie said. "He's Kuma's friend, and he's a pother. He might be able to help with the injured sheep."

Yuli raised her eyebrows. "The one they've been searching for?"

Raffa held his breath as Yuli looked him over.

"Hmph," she said. "You're with Kuma, and you're

a healer. Tell me what you need. If I have it, it's yours."

Then she nodded, and Raffa could breathe again.

Missum Yuli helped him make four poultices—two for healing, one to stop bleeding, and one to ease pain. He thanked her and delivered them to Uncle Elson. With the morning nearly gone, he saw Kuma coming out of the henhouse and called to her.

"Will you come with me?" he said.

He wanted a look at the grain storage sheds. The crows had attacked neither people nor animals, yet he was certain that they were not ordinary birds. Why would they have landed at the sheds and done nothing?

As they walked across the common area, Kuma drew a long, shaky breath. "It could have been worse," she said. "They got more than half the chickens—that's a lot, but no one will go hungry."

They drew near the storage sheds. Raffa saw that each shed was built with a gap under the eaves to allow air to circulate. The first shed was filled with field corn for animal feed. He thought back to the attack. The crows hadn't landed at this shed, so he and Kuma walked on to the next one.

The second shed held wheat. Inside, the space was partitioned into several bins by walls higher than Raffa's head. The bins were open at the top, and each had a half door in one of its walls. When the bins were full after fall harvest, the settlers could climb a ladder to get to the grain through the opening at the top.

Now the bins were partially depleted, the grain about knee-high. Raffa opened one of the half doors and looked inside. He saw two small cloth sacks atop the grain, each about the size of his palm. They were open at one end, and he could tell by their limpness that they were empty.

"Odd upon strange," he muttered.

He tried to make a picture in his head. The crows had landed under the eaves and entered the shed through the gap. They must have dropped these little sacks into the grain bins and then flown off.

He ducked through the door, picked up the two sacks, and handed them to Kuma, while he checked two of the other bins. The same sacks in each. A sense of dread was growing in his stomach.

Kuma looked inside one of the sacks. "Empty," she said.

She tried the second one—and cried out. "No! Oh, no!"

"What? What is it?"

She inverted the sack over her open palm. A weevil fell into her hand.

Raffa stared at it as comprehension knifed through him.

The sacks had been full of weevils: The bins were now infested with thousands of the voracious, destructive insects. Many of them had no doubt already laid eggs, not only in the wheat but in the cracks and crevices of the bins themselves.

The wheat would be all but ruined. And the sheds would be unusable until after next winter, when the freezing weather would kill off the weevils and their eggs.

Kuma's lips were pale, and she was trembling. "I was wrong," she whispered. "Now people *will* go hungry."

They hurried back to the big barn and found Elson. Immediately a group was organized to begin sieving the grain in an attempt to salvage what they could.

Raffa berated himself silently. *We should have gotten here sooner. We waited too long in the Suddens—if I'd made up my mind quicker, I'd be home by now, and Mam and Da—*

His thoughts were interrupted by mutters and grumbles, and he looked up to see some of the steaders casting unfriendly glances at him.

What had he done to anger them?

One of the men strode forward and pointed at Raffa. "You there—who are you, and what are you doing here?"

Elson stepped toward the group, whose hostility seemed to crackle through the air.

"He's a friend," Elson said, looking from face to face.

"Yah?" the man said, challenge in his voice. "Known him long?"

Elson didn't answer directly. "If you have something to say, Bantan, say it."

Bantan raised his chin. "He's the one told us all to cover our eyes. We done it, and nothing happened. But that's when the stoats got in. Like he was helping them."

Rumbles of agreement from other steaders.

"He's a pother," Bantan went on. "Those weren't normal beasts. A pother could have . . . done something to them, to make them act so."

Raffa stared at Bantan, so stunned he couldn't speak.

Kuma managed to stammer, "No, you—you— That's not—"

"Steady on," Elson said. "He worked side by side with us, fighting the foxes the whole time. Some of you surely saw him. And yes, he's a pother. He made poultices for the wounded sheep."

Bantan jutted out his chin. "Could be covering his tracks, I say. Because it's beyond odd for a stranger to show up just when all this happens."

His words triggered a buzz among the other steaders.

"That's right."

"Who is he, anyway?"

"—chickens dead, because of him."

They think I'm part of it!

Raffa's mind could hardly grasp what was happening. The irony would have been laughable had it not been so grim: Here he was doing everything he could to combat the Chancellor's dread project, and instead he was suspected of abetting it.

Worst of all, Bantan was right—although not in the way he thought. Raffa *had* been part of the Chancellor's plot earlier, when he knew almost nothing about it. He winced to recall how eager and excited he had been about being invited to participate.

Now, because of that error, he was determined to work twice as hard to right things and prove his worth, not only to Bantan and the others but to himself.

Elson walked over to Raffa and put an arm around his shoulders. "Come, Raffa. It's time for sunpeak meal." He glared at each person in the group, Bantan last. "This young man is a guest in my home. He is a friend of our Kuma. Doubt him and you doubt me."

Elson's words seemed to dissipate the tension. As he walked Raffa toward the house, some of the steaders returned to their work.

But Raffa could still feel Bantan's stare stabbing into his back.

CHAPTER TEN

B EWILDERMENT, anger, helplessness—all roiled through Raffa. He felt almost dizzy and stumbled on a stone; Elson caught his arm and righted him as they walked from the barns back toward the house.

"Kuma, did you ever tell Raffa how the settlement got started?" Elson asked.

Raffa looked at him in confusion. Elson's tone was totally relaxed, as if they were conversing during a leisurely stroll.

"No, I never did," Kuma answered, looking equally surprised.

"Raffa, most of us are descended from Afters," Elson

said. "Our ancestors traveled to Obsidia together after the Great Quake. They found no work in Gilden, so they decided to farm instead. None of them had farmed before. The first years were lean indeed."

He shook his head as if he had lived through those times himself. "But we learned. We're still learning. I wish we could say we've prospered since then. That wouldn't be true—it's a struggle yet. Most years, though, we have enough food to eat, and enough cheer to sing and tell tales in the evenings."

They had reached the house by now, where Haddie heard the last of what Elson said and chimed in, smiling, "A body doesn't need more than that."

Elson had succeeded in distracting Raffa. "My ancestors were Afters, too," he said. "Not my mam's family, but the Santanas, on my da's side."

"Santana!" Haddie exclaimed. "Kuma, you never said!"

Kuma tilted her head. "Said what?"

"But surely you know—the Santanas are famous among the Afters!" Haddie beamed at Raffa. "There would be no califer plants in Obsidia if it weren't for them. Why, who knows how much suffering has been banished because of califerium!"

"Their abilities as well," Elson added. "Your ancestors and the other apothecaries who came from afar were more skilled than Obsidia's native healers. No telling how many lives were saved because of the knowledge they brought and shared."

A small flush of pride warmed Raffa inside and rose to his cheeks. Elson and Haddie had helped remind him who he was. That was where he had to put his time and mind and muscle—no matter what anyone else thought of him.

They sat down for a quick meal of cold flat corn cakes and hot tea. Elson looked solemn.

"Last night, after everything you told us, I wondered if there were a reasonable explanation," he said. "I seek one no longer." He bowed his head toward both Raffa and Kuma in apology.

A wave of regret and sorrow washed over Raffa. The attack proved that he and Kuma had been telling the truth—but at such a dire cost to the settlement. He would far rather have answered a thousand doubtful questions from Elson.

The Chancellor was using the animals against people. Not enemies of Obsidia but *her own people*.

"We're the farthest settlement," Kuma said. "It's a good distance from here to Gilden." Her words came slowly, each one burdened with thought.

"Yes?" Haddie prompted her gently.

Kuma looked at Raffa. "I think it—it was a kind of experiment," she said. "They're testing the animals. Out here, so people in Gilden won't know about it."

"And that's why the guards left!" Raffa exclaimed. "So no one would tie them to the attack."

Elson shook his head. "I am trying to think of what to say . . . to everyone, that they will believe."

"Whether or not they believe," Haddie said, "the question they will ask is, What's next? And, What do we do now?"

Raffa put his hands to his head as if to tear his hair out, overcome with hopelessness. He had been sure upon certain about the crows—and he'd been wrong. It was beyond impossible to predict what other terrors might be inflicted using the animals.

Then he heard the faint sound of a dog barking. Everyone tensed and turned their heads toward the sound.

"It's only the one," Haddie said immediately.

"Still," Elson said, and he rose from his seat. They

all followed him outside, where he grabbed an ax. Kuma took up a shovel, Raffa a pitchfork, and Haddie a hoe.

The barks were coming from across the fields behind the house. No one else seemed to have heard them. As they approached the hedgerow, Raffa could see the dog, a white coat, brown spots, a brush of a tail.

The dog had discovered something in the hedge. Elson made a quick gesture with his hand. The dog stopped barking and backed away a few steps but remained alert, ears pricked.

Haddie prodded the undergrowth aside with the hoe.

"A fox," she announced. "It's wounded."

With Kuma at his side, Raffa knelt down for a closer look. The fox was a male. Its torso was soaked with blood, and one of its hind legs was badly lacerated. The injured creature raised its head for a moment. Its eyes were wild with pain.

And they were *purple*.

"Best to end its suffering," Elson said.

"No!" Kuma jumped to her feet. "Uncle, it's not his fault! We have to help him!" Without waiting for a response, she turned to Raffa. "You can, can't you? Treat him and heal him?"

Raffa was already going over botanical combinations

in his head. He realized—with surprise and a little pride—that it had become a natural reflex for him on seeing injury or illness.

"I can try," he said.

Haddie took Kuma's hands in hers. "Child, listen to me. You know that there are those who already have doubts about your friend. If they should find out that we've rescued this creature and that he's treating it . . . I fear what they might do in anger."

Raffa's eyes widened. He was shaken to his core: How could healing ever be seen as anything but an act for good?

Kuma glanced at him quickly. "Then we'll keep it a secret," she said. She turned and began running back toward the house, calling over her shoulder, "I'll get a board and some sacking."

Elson and Haddie exchanged looks of resignation. Haddie sighed. "Would you expect any different from a girl who keeps company with a bear?"

Kuma spoke quietly to the fox and managed to tie its muzzle with a rag. She then slipped the sacking under it. Elson and Raffa helped slide the sacking onto the board and carried the fox across the fields.

There was a shed at the side of the dooryard, used for storing tools and firewood. Haddie cleared off a shelf in the shed, after stating plainly that Kuma would not be permitted to bring the fox into the house. They put the board on the shelf.

Kuma cleaned the fox's fur and found the source of the bleeding: a single ragged puncture in its midsection, probably from a pitchfork. Raffa sorted through his meager store of botanicals. Missum Yuli had shared her ingredients, but she had nothing like the variety a practiced apothecary would have.

Raffa made a combination based on spineflower root, which was used to treat puncture wounds. He still had the dried scarlet-vine powder. It hadn't worked for Echo, but Raffa wondered if that was because of the primitive conditions at the mountain shelter, where he hadn't been able to prepare infusions properly. Kuma's house was no laboratory, but at least he could improvise some equipment from kitchen utensils.

After steeping and straining the powder, he pounded it into the spineflower combination. Sure enough, he saw a few sparks and glimmers. Nothing as spectacular as when he used the fresh vine, but still promising. He decided to use spineflower again in a different combination for an infusion, and added the vine powder to that as well.

As he continued to pound, he saw the glimmers inside his head as well as with his eyes. It was all but impossible to describe, but each glint in the mortar matched a point of light in his mind. Raffa recognized the sensation: It was his instinctive ability for apothecary. His intuition was telling him that he was on the right path.

So I haven't lost it after all, he thought with a sigh of relief.

Then he paused, his mind lit by new awareness. Apothecary was like anything else: It took regular practice to remain adept. In the Suddens, his skills had grown stiff and rusty with underuse. When he made that infusion for Echo, he'd felt nothing but blankness. And sure enough, the infusion had been ineffective.

In that moment, Raffa truly grasped for the first time his father's cautions against depending on instinct. It was only through experience and study and learning that he would be able to reliably interpret those mysterious moments of intuition. I need to learn to use it like a tool, he thought, not a—a crutch for leaning on.

Feeling both grateful and humbled, Raffa took the infusion to the woodshed to dose the fox. He couldn't even get close: With a surge of fear-driven strength, the animal writhed and lunged at him. Raffa jerked away, almost spilling the infusion.

"Let me help," Kuma said.

Perhaps it was her soothing voice. Or maybe the fox sensed somehow that she had been his savior from the start. Whatever the reason, he lay quiet for Kuma, allowing her to remove the muzzle-rag. She held him still while Raffa administered the infusion. Then he applied the poultice to both the puncture wound and the lacerated leg.

Kuma bound the wounds with strips of linen. She squeezed some water from a rag into the fox's mouth. Raffa helped her lift the board into a box, which they covered with more sacking.

By the time they finished, the fox was asleep.

Raffa peered beneath the eaves at the back of the house. It didn't take him long to locate Echo, hanging in a corner fast asleep. The bat was so small and inconspicuous, no one else except perhaps Kuma could have spotted him.

On Elson's advice, Raffa stayed away from the settlement that afternoon. He walked the meadows and hedgerows gathering botanica. As always, the search for useful plants occupied and soothed his unsettled mind. To his delight, he found panax plants, whose roots were a powerful stimulant. He was also able to replenish his supply of several other botanicals, including phosphorescent fungi, and he filled a bag with nettle tops, thinking that Elson or Haddie might like to cook them.

In midafternoon, he headed back. As the house came into view, he saw Kuma waving both arms at him. He broke into a trot. When he drew within earshot, she called out to him.

"The fox," she said. "I think he's waking up."

They crossed the yard. Kuma opened the door to the shed. The sacking atop the box was moving. As they watched, the fox tried to find his way out from under, but he succeeded only in pulling the sacking into the box.

"You mustn't get yourself tangled," Kuma said. She eased the sacking off.

Raffa stood back a step, not wanting the fox to get agitated on seeing him.

The fox stared up at Kuma, his eyes purest purple.

"Red . . . spring!" the fox said.

He looked, as foxes so often did, like he was smiling.

"Red spring! Red spring!" the fox repeated.

Raffa's mouth gaped in shock. It had been many months since an infusion of the scarlet vine had caused an animal to talk—first Echo, then the baby raccoons, Twig and her brother, Bando. He realized that he had never expected it to happen again.

Kuma, too, had been stunned motionless. Now she recovered and said, "What do you think he means?"

Red spring? Raffa shook his head. He had heard of spring fever and spring chickens, but never of a red spring. . . .

Then an idea occurred to him. He hurried to the corner of the house where Echo was sleeping under the eaves.

"Echo? Would you come with me, please?" He tapped gently on the edge of the cave.

Echo stirred, stretched his wings partway open, and closed them again. Then he fluttered to the perch necklace.

Raffa brought the bat to the shed.

"Red . . . spring!" the fox said.

"Fox talk," Echo said.

"Yes, Echo, he's talking. Do you know what he's saying?"

"Fox say . . ." Echo paused. "Fox say, red spring."

Kuma swallowed a smile. Raffa rolled his eyes and tried again. "Thank you, Echo, I heard what he said. Do you know what he *means* by that?"

"Fox red," Echo replied.

Raffa took a breath to tighten his grip on his patience, which was beginning to feel quite slippery. "That's right. He's a red fox."

Echo clicked, a sign that he was annoyed. "Bat *Echo*," he said. "Fox *Red*."

"His name!" Kuma exclaimed. "Echo, are you saying that Red is his name?"

"Kuma good!" Echo squeaked.

Red, spring.

Raffa frowned, thinking hard. The phrase reminded him of something. . . . What was it? He gnawed on a knuckle—why wouldn't it come to him?

The smell of supper cooking drifted out into the yard. Raffa blinked.

Food. It had something to do with food.

Then he knew.

Months earlier. Dinner in Gilden with the Chancellor, where she had demonstrated the results of the first attempts to train the animals.

"It's a command!" he exclaimed. "The Chancellor at

dinner—when she called the chickadees, she said, 'Beak, deliver!' And the crows, 'Ink, deliver!' All of them have the same name—"

In Kuma's eyes, he saw what he was feeling: a terrible moment of understanding.

Spring—at the throats of the sheep. And at the chickens on their roosts.

Red, spring!

It was the command that had sent the foxes to attack.

The fox was now trying to get out of the box. "Red spring, red spring, red spring red spring red—"

In a spate of frenzy, his front paws scrabbled desperately at nothing. Then he began jerking his head back and forth while at the same time snapping his jaws.

"Why is he doing that?" Kuma said in distress. She picked up the sacking and tried to wrap the fox in it. "Shusss, shusss."

The fox let out a single yap so sharp and desperate that it was more like a scream. Then his eyes glazed over and he fell back, unconscious.

CHAPTER ELEVEN

K UMA gasped. "What's the matter with him?"

Raffa was as puzzled as she was. The fox's jerky twitching seemed familiar, but he couldn't quite place it.

Now that the animal had lost consciousness, Raffa was able to examine him carefully. "It looks like the puncture is a flesh wound. I don't think any of the organs got damaged."

The bleeding had stopped, and both wounds were clean and dry. The scarlet vine had again worked its miracle. Two of them: the healing, and the speaking.

Raffa narrowed his eyes, trying to concentrate.

Hundreds of animals in the Chancellor's secret com-pound had been dosed with a combination containing the vine, yet, as far as he knew, none of them could speak. Only four had gained that ability—

The ones he himself had treated.

Raffa's heart thumped in his chest. *Can it be . . . Is it because of* me?

Ever since Raffa was a small child, people had regarded his apothecarial talent with awe. In fact, many in the pother settlement called him "the baby genius," which he had always hated. Now he found himself won-dering if they might have been right all along.

A bat, two raccoons, and a fox.

He had treated them.

Raffa's pride swelled as his thoughts raced. He had known from the start that the scarlet vine was special, but now it seemed that it wasn't just the vine itself.

It was him.

He squared his shoulders and lifted his chin. It would be a great responsibility: He alone would have the power to decide which animals were to be given the gift of speech. Perhaps working animals should take priority over pets. His parents would surely help him make these kinds of decisions at first. . . .

His parents.

He heard their voices in his head, reminding him what it meant to be an honorable apothecary, whose first duty was always to heal.

And the sentence shifted.

He had *treated* them.

Raffa froze as realization pushed its way through his bloated pride.

Each of the four animals had been badly injured. Somehow, when given to a *wounded* animal, the scarlet vine had the wondrous consequence of enabling it to speak. None of the creatures in the secret shed compound could talk . . . because they had been dosed while healthy.

Raffa knew in his bones that this was the truth, and he had to close his eyes for a moment in utter embarrassment, beyond grateful that he'd spoken none of his thoughts aloud.

It wasn't him at all.

Chastened, he returned his attention to the fox. He was now completely limp, not asleep, but in a deep state of torpor.

Kuma hovered over the box, her face tight with

worry. "He . . . It reminds me of when Echo was sick, remember?"

How could he forget? Raffa reached for the perch to stroke Echo with a fingertip, with silent thanks for the bat's recovery.

Haddie came out to the yard to announce that supper would be late. All hands were needed to erect torch stands throughout the common area. Elson and the other settlement leaders were hoping that torches burning through the night would discourage any further attacks.

Raffa wanted to help, but once again Elson thought it best that he stay out of sight and mind of the other steaders. Elson had met with the heads of the settlement families that afternoon to tell them of the Chancellor's plot. As expected, the responses ranged from skepticism to downright disbelief, but all were agreed on the importance of stopping another attack.

"I couldn't leave your name out of the telling," Elson said. "I'm afraid Bantan is all the more suspicious now. I'd rather not have to worry about you getting into trouble with anyone tonight."

Raffa had to concede that Elson was speaking sense. Besides, staying behind would give him a chance to work on trying to cure the fox.

With Haddie's permission, he used one end of the table as a workspace. As he cleared the table, he thought about the fox, his state of torpor so like that which had afflicted Echo.

Suddenly a brilliant white light filled his mind, so strong that he blinked against its brightness. It lasted only a few moments, and as it faded, Raffa realized why it had come to him.

The cavern plant! I'll make a stimulant, with the cavern plant added!

Missum Yuli had given him some mellia and dried ranagua berries. He also had the panax root he had found that afternoon. He would combine those three botanicals with the cavern plant. If it worked, it would be an important step toward confirming that the cavern plant did indeed have healing properties.

The plant's twiggy growth had a smooth surface that felt slightly waxy to the touch. Raffa knew of other water plants with this quality—lily pads, sea-celery, bubbleweed. Useful water plants were boiled to extract their essences, and then the solution was boiled further until only a residue remained.

It was a tricky procedure. There was nothing quite as mind-numbingly tedious as watching a liquid boil. In a single moment of inattentiveness, the solution could go from boil to burn, ruining the residue.

Raffa came up with a way to attend to the solution while keeping boredom at bay. He played a game with Echo, the bat's favorite. It was very simple: They took turns naming insects. The first one to repeat an insect named earlier was the loser.

"Skeeto," Echo said.

"Midge."

"Mayfly."

Raffa set up a pattern: Each time he named an insect, he checked the solution. "Katydid."

"Wasp."

"Skimmer."

"Moonwing."

"Moonwing?" Raffa shook his head. "I've never heard of that—are you making it up?"

Then he checked himself. Of course Echo would know insects that Raffa himself wasn't familiar with. Besides, was it even possible for the bat to make things up? Animals were capable of deception, he knew; they could hide from predators or feign injury. *But that's different from . . . from inventing things. Or lying.*

Only humans, it seemed, had that dubious ability.

"Moonwing tasty," Echo chirped.

"I'll take your word for it," Raffa replied. He wondered what a moonwing looked like.

The game went on for a surprisingly long time. It never failed to amaze Raffa, the number of flying insects Echo could name.

It was Raffa's turn. "Mayfly."

"Raffa no! Echo mayfly! Echo win! Echo good!"

Echo always won. Fair and square, too—Raffa never "let" him win. The bat was surprised and delighted when he triumphed, no matter how many times it happened.

After three rounds of the game—with Echo winning all three—the solution had nearly boiled dry. Raffa took the pot from the stove; the last of the liquid evaporated from the heat of the pot alone. He let the pot cool a little, then carefully scraped a portion of the residue into his mortar.

He pounded the ingredients together until they were powdered. He added a few drops of colza oil, then began working the pestle with a circular motion. So familiar, this action . . . taking him to a place that was somehow apart from the rest of the world, a place where he could empty his troubled mind of everything except the work. It was here, in this state, that he had experienced his strongest moments of intuition. Would it happen this time?

Soon he had a smooth paste; he stopped moving the pestle to take a closer look.

To his amazement, the paste continued to spin!

Quickly he lifted the mortar off the tabletop. Untouched, the paste was still swirling and spinning, a hollow in its center, like a tiny, perfect whirlpool. He stared at it, mesmerized.

And in his mind, he heard a humming noise whose cadence was round and even and steady upon solid.

Raffa took the infusion out to the shed, along with a lantern, which he hung from a nail in the wall. He placed two fingers on the fox's chest. The beats of his heart were far apart, just as Echo's had been. But his wounds had healed so well that Raffa decided to remove the bindings.

He dosed the fox with the cavern-plant infusion. There was nothing to do now but wait.

Echo flitted off to hunt. Raffa spent the next couple of hours cleaning and sorting the botanicals he had collected that afternoon. Then Kuma arrived, her face smeared with soot. "The torches are ready," she said.

"And we're divided into two shifts, to stand watch. Elson and Haddie and I are on the second shift."

Raffa hoped that Elson would allow him to help stand watch; maybe he could be posted where Bantan wouldn't see him.

"I dosed him earlier," he said, nodding toward the fox. "I might have to give him more than one—"

"Raffa, look!"

The fox was awake. He pawed at the sacking until it fell off. Then he stood up in the box. Kuma took a step toward him; he growled and bared his teeth.

She moved no closer, but spoke quietly to Raffa. "His eyes," she said.

Raffa looked at the fox's face. His eyes were completely black, without the faintest trace of purple.

The animal drew back from them, growling and bristling. Whatever he did seemed natural and normal; his movements were no longer jerky or manic.

"Stand up, slowly," Kuma said. "I think he can get to the floor by jumping down on that crate. I'm going to open the door. Be prepared for him to bolt." She backed away, the fox watching her every move.

Raffa rose and edged toward the wall. Kuma threw open the door. The fox jumped out of the box. He leapt from the shelf to the crate, then practically flew through the door, a rust-colored blur.

They rushed outside the shed and watched as the fox dashed across the field and disappeared from sight.

Kuma's eyes were shining. "Did you see that?" she exclaimed. She held out her hands toward Raffa, palms flat and together, and he clapped her hands between his.

"You did it!" she said. "He's his lovely wild self again!"

They returned to the house. Kuma chattered on about the fox; Raffa didn't think he'd ever seen her so animated. He finally cut in; he had something important to discuss with her.

". . . and the injuries all healed, too—"

"You heard him growl, didn't you?" he asked.

"Yes, he sounded completely normal!"

"Do you think that means he can't talk now?"

She looked at him in surprise. "I didn't think of that," she said. "But it makes sense, doesn't it?"

Raffa nodded slowly. It *did* make sense—which was why he couldn't bring himself to voice his next thoughts. Given what had happened to the fox, could Echo likewise lose his ability to speak?

Maybe . . . I could give him a tiny dose of the scar-let-vine infusion. To keep him talking. Raffa felt the wrongness of this impulse like a pebble in his shoe, but he couldn't help thinking about it.

Kuma's eyes widened. "You're worried about Echo, aren't you," she said in a near-whisper. "You're afraid that he might stop talking, too."

"I don't understand it," Raffa said. "He ate those insects in the cavern two days ago, but he can still speak."

Kuma wrinkled her forehead. "Listen to what you just said. Echo ate the insects. The fox had the infusion. Maybe that's the difference."

Raffa lifted his head in sudden hope. That, too, made sense. The essence distilled from the cavern plant and then combined with the other botanicals might well have a different effect from the insects. He shouldn't assume that Echo would stop talking; for the time being, he should watch and wait.

But what if Echo wants to stop talking—and doesn't want to stay with me anymore?

Raffa recalled that Echo had clearly enjoyed meeting the bats in the cavern, and had once spoken wistfully about the companionship of other bats.

He's not a prisoner, Raffa thought stubbornly. He

can leave anytime. He's staying with me because he wants to.

Kuma was studying his face. "It could be like with me and Roo," she said, "her living in the wild, but I can still see her whenever I want."

Once again she had seemingly read his mind, and he understood what she had left unsaid. She would far rather that Echo reverted entirely to his natural, wild, nonspeaking self.

Raffa couldn't bring himself to think about life without Echo's daily companionship. To his relief, Kuma changed the subject.

"Haddie says we're to eat," she said. "They're still working. They'll come home when they can."

He was grateful for the change in subject, and gave her a silent nod of thanks.

She dished out corn mush. Raffa ate quickly, not really noticing the food, his mind on the fox again.

He had finally remembered where he had seen something like the fox's twitchiness: in a very few patients treated by his parents. Patients who had misused their botanical combinations, by taking them for too long a time or in too great a quantity. They became addicted. Their hands shook; their movements were jerky; they developed facial tics. They took more and more of the infusion but gained less and less relief. It was a terrible, crippling cycle.

Raffa was reminded of a conversation with Uncle Ansel about the dosing of the animals. *It wears off. . . . They have to be dosed for every training session.*

So perhaps the fox had been given the vine infusion over and over. Echo had not shown any signs of addiction, but he had been dosed only a few times.

The symptoms of addiction . . . the state of torpor. Could both be caused by the vine, the one from overuse, the other a long-term repercussion? The vine was such an unknown botanical, and Raffa's father, Mohan, had cautioned him about it from the very beginning. *There is too much we do not know*, Mohan had said.

While still not a certainty, it seemed highly likely that the cavern plant had the ability to counteract the negative effects of the scarlet vine: Just as eating the insects had cured Echo, the combination with the cavern plant had cured the fox and returned him to his natural state. For a brief moment, Raffa wished that they hadn't released the fox; he would have liked to observe him for a few days, to see if the cure was permanent.

But besides the fact that Kuma wouldn't have stood

for it, the idea of keeping the fox in captivity made Raffa think once again of the hundreds of trapped animals in the secret shed compound. . . .

A flash of realization made him sit up straighter. Releasing the animals in the compound would accomplish two things in one shake: It would stop the Chancellor's project, and it would give the animals their freedom.

But Raffa knew that he couldn't uncage them as they were now, dosed with the vine. It made them docile and obedient, and suppressed many of their natural instincts.

If he could somehow manage to feed the antidote to all the animals in the shed compound, so that they would return to their normal state, and *then* free them— that was the answer!

"Kuma," he said, his voice low and tense. "I think the scarlet-vine infusion might be producing bad effects as well as good ones. But the cavern plant could be an antidote. What I want to do now is to make a whole lot of the antidote, and then—"

"Wait," she said. "You think *the vine* might be what made Echo sick? And the fox as well?"

"I can't be sure, but it seems likely—"

"So it could be that any animal dosed with the vine might get sick?"

"There's no way of knowing," Raffa said, shaking his head, "without examining them. Two cases—that's not enough to be certain."

"But . . ." Her forehead creased in worry. "Don't you see what that means, for Twig? If it's true, then she might be sick now, too!"

CHAPTER TWELVE

R AFFA immediately tried to reassure Kuma. "She wasn't dosed anywhere near as many times as the fox," he said.

"Neither was Echo," she retorted. "Raffa, she's barely more than a baby! It might affect her differently. I have to go back and see how she is. And take some of the antidote with me."

He argued a little longer, but nothing he said alleviated her fears. She insisted that they immediately begin work on the antidote. Raffa agreed; he wanted to do this anyway.

He decided to make the combination a powder; it

would be easier to carry that way. By using every single pot and pan in the house, he was able to convert the entire stock of cavern plants. Then he mixed the residue with the other botanicals, and ground them together until he thought his arm would fall off. His skills might well be a little rusty, but he was quickly regaining his confidence: It felt good to be focused on apothecary work again.

Kuma helped by fetching and clearing away. They ended up with a sack of powder, and set aside a small pouchful for Twig.

With the antidote powder finished, Raffa attended to one more task: distilling the phosphorescent fungi so he could use their essence for lightsticks. He had made the fungi combination so many times that he could have done it in his sleep.

"Aunt and Uncle should be back soon," Kuma said. "They'll be hungry." She stirred up the mush on the stove.

"I've been meaning to ask you something about them," Raffa said. "You told me that they don't care about you. I don't understand—ever since we got here, they've been nothing but caring."

Kuma went still for a long moment, the wooden

spoon in her hand forgotten. Then she shrugged. "You haven't seen what it's usually like. The children haven't been here. It's usually noisy and crowded and . . . and it's obvious that they don't need one more person around to worry about."

Raffa stared at her. Odd upon strange, he thought, that someone so sensitive to animals and other people could be so blind about her own life. He spoke gently. "Did you ever think that maybe they don't want to get in your way? I think they know how much you love the Forest, and Roo, and they don't want to interfere. That's why they let you go off, and why they don't ask you to explain yourself. Not because they don't care, but because they *do*."

Another shrug. "I don't know about that," she said.

Her voice was doubtful, but Raffa thought he saw a flicker in her eyes. Of hope, maybe, or at least interest. He decided not to press further.

"Well, you might think on it," he said lightly. "Anyway, I mustn't forget to thank them. They've been more than welcoming to me."

Having finished extracting the fungi essence, he returned his thoughts to a more pressing problem.

"We have to figure out a way to dose all the animals,"

he said. "Maybe Trixin could help us. After that, we'll go back to the gorge for Twig—"

"*What?*" Kuma almost yelped. "What are you talking about?" She held up the little pouch. "I'm leaving to go to Twig right now!"

Raffa frowned. "Kuma, you saw what happened here in your own settlement. The Chancellor is using the animals against *people*. Who knows when the next attack will be? We have to get to those animals *now*."

Kuma shook her head, her lips set in a straight line. "Going to the gorge first will only delay us a little—a couple of days at the most."

What was the matter with her? She clearly wasn't thinking straight. "You said it yourself," he replied. "People are going to go hungry here, and it could happen again and again unless we stop it! How can you put one single life ahead of hundreds?"

"It's not just Twig!" she snapped. "I'm thinking of Roo as well. Do you know how heartbroken she'll be if Twig dies? That's *two* lives—" She held up two fingers and thrust them toward him. "*Two* that I care about!"

"'Be kind to animals, kinder to people,'" Raffa retorted, quoting a familiar saying, one he was sure Kuma knew.

"Don't you dare," Kuma said, her eyes blazing. "What if it were Echo? We left the Suddens because he was sick!"

Raffa stiffened and goggled at her like a fish.

She's right, he thought.

But he immediately began arguing with himself. *No—it's not the same! We don't even know if Twig is sick!*

It didn't matter. Just five words—*What if it were Echo?*—had changed how he felt.

He swallowed. "Okay. You have to go. I see that now. But you know how hard it's going to be in Gilden. I'll need your help."

Kuma began collecting things to pack for her journey. "When you get there, you'll have to find out what's going on and make a plan," she said. "I'll be there in time to help. I want to free those animals, too, you know. As much as you do." A pause. "Maybe more."

"When will you get there? Where will we meet?"

"I—I'll find Garith. Or Trixin. And I'll get a message to you."

"Kuma, I—"

All those months in the Suddens, living with her and Garith, never seeing another human soul . . . Garith was already gone. Now Raffa would be separated from Kuma as well, and he realized how much he had come to depend on her companionship.

"What?"

"Just come as quick as you can, okay?"

Their eyes met for a solemn moment, and he knew that they understood each other.

Elson and Haddie walked in. Haddie looked from Kuma to Raffa, apparently sensing the tension between them. "Have you eaten?" she asked.

"Yes," Raffa and Kuma answered in unison.

"Good," Elson said. If he noticed anything amiss, he was choosing to ignore it, for he went on with some urgency. "Raffa, I'm sorry, but I think it best that you leave here tonight. Do you have somewhere you can go?"

"Shakes and tremors, don't frighten the lad!" Haddie admonished her husband. She bustled around the table and put her hands on Raffa's shoulders. "We just heard that a fox was spotted earlier," she said, "in the fields back of the settlement."

Raffa and Kuma exchanged a quick glance. The chances were better than good that it was *their* fox.

"It's got everyone wobbled," Elson said. "They're all

on the lookout for foxes and stoats and crows."

"Oh, no!" Kuma cried out. "Did you tell them about the purple eyes? You have to tell them! They can't go around hurting animals that are normal!"

"I told them," Elson replied. "And I'll remind them again."

He paced the room in obvious agitation. "It was the loss of grain that did it—the fear about whether their families will have enough to eat. Fear on top of anger—a bad combination. Doesn't leave any room for reason."

He turned to Raffa. "The fox that was just sighted, if someone manages to capture it, they'll see its scars, and how well the fox has healed, and they'll suspect you right away. And if it *wasn't* your fox, are there more in hiding? Could there be another attack tonight? I don't want you around here. I'm worried for your safety—that someone will do something worse than foolish."

It should have been all the same to Raffa—he needed to go anyway. But being forced to leave made him feel much worse than if he had chosen to do so freely.

"I—I'm going on to Gilden," he said, "but I'm going to the pother settlement first."

"I'll take you part of the way in the wagon," Elson said. "It's the least I can do, to make up for being so inhospitable. But I'll need to be back in time for our turn on watch."

"I'm leaving, too," Kuma announced, "as soon as our watch shift is over."

"Oh, Kuma, we only just got you back!" Haddie said in dismay. "Must you go?"

"I wouldn't if I didn't have to," Kuma said. "I promise that if it's within my powers, I won't be gone as long this time."

Haddie sighed. "I don't like it. Not one bit. With all that's happening around here . . . Is it that bear again?"

"No," Kuma answered. "It's a raccoon. A baby one."

"And after that she's going on to Gilden, to meet me there," Raffa said loudly, with a pointed glance at Kuma.

"In that case, you'll stop home in between," Haddie declared, "if only for a night." She stared first at Kuma and then at Raffa, as if daring them to argue with her.

Raffa wanted Kuma to join him sooner rather than later, but he said nothing. It was up to her to decide. Besides, after the way he had encouraged her to think about her family, and after all the kindness they had shown him, he could hardly object.

Haddie gave Kuma a quick hug and released her with

a smack to her bottom. Then she began scurrying from cupboard to table.

"Neither of you is setting a foot outside this door," she said, "until I pack a full tucker for you."

To Raffa's relief, Echo returned from hunting in time to board the wagon with him. Elson made sure to hail several neighbors as he drove out of the settlement with Raffa in plain sight on the wagon seat.

"There," he said. "Now word is sure to get back to Bantan that you were seen leaving."

As they rode, they talked about the Chancellor and her allies. "What could they possibly be trying to accomplish?" Elson wondered.

Raffa had had months to ponder that question, yet he had no answers. "I know that what happened last night was terrible," he said slowly, "but there are so many animals in that compound. What you saw was only a tiny part of it. They've got to be planning something much bigger than the attack here."

His stomach tightened in anxiety. He tried to comfort himself with the thought that he didn't actually need to know. That was part of the logic of his plot to free the animals. It didn't matter what the Chancellor's plan was: Releasing the animals would thwart it.

Raffa had been to the shed compound twice. A sturdy fence topped with nails and broken glass surrounded it. The gate was guarded day and night, and since he and Kuma had managed to free Roo, it was sure to be even more heavily guarded now.

As the wagon bumped along through the cold, damp spring evening, Raffa's doubts began to grow. If making a good plan was hard, carrying it out was a thousand times harder. And the closer he got to Gilden, the more impossible his task appeared.

In the Eastern Woodlands, a little farther than halfway to the pother settlement, Elson turned the wagon off the road and followed a smaller track. It ended in a clearing just large enough to turn the horses. In the moonlight, Raffa saw a tiny cabin, and as he jumped down from the wagon seat, he could hear the gurgle of a stream.

"Wayfarer shelter," Elson said. "I'll be easier in mind if you stay the night here. When you go back to the main trail, keep heading north. When it forks, go left for the ferry, right for the pother settlement."

The ride had saved Raffa several hours of walking.

If he left here at daybirth, he would reach home by late afternoon.

Inside the cabin there was a rough bunk and a small fireplace with wood already laid. Elson lingered in the doorway.

"I'm sorry again that I couldn't do better to convince Bantan and the other doubters," he said.

Raffa was silent for a moment. "*You* believed us," he said. "That means . . . more than I could ever say."

He'd been a stranger to Elson—a kiddler with an outlandish story. Elson might have doubted him at first, but not anymore, and his trust was a gift without price for Raffa.

Elson held up his hand, and Raffa matched palms with him. "Truth loves the light, Raffa," Elson said. "It never stays buried forever. Bantan and the rest will see it soon enough. You'll always be welcome in our home."

"Thank you," Raffa whispered, "for everything."

The next morning was misty and gray. Raffa rose eagerly. This was the day he would see his parents again!

He cleaned the ashes from the little fireplace, then gathered wood and laid it for the next wayfarer. In the packet of food Haddie had given him was a corn cake folded around a scrape of butter, which he ate as he walked.

The road wound through forest and brush, and Raffa normally would have been on the lookout for botanicals. Today, though, keen to reach home, he alternated between trotting and a fast walk. His quick pace joggled the perch necklace, and Echo occasionally clicked in irritation.

Raffa left the road well before it reached the edge of the woodlands. His home lay just outside the pother settlement; Mohan and Salima had built on a patch of land big enough for an extensive garden.

Mindful of the guards at Kuma's settlement, Raffa pulled out the perch necklace and blew on Echo's whiskers. "Echo, I'm sorry to have to wake you now. I need you to fly ahead again, and see if anyone's there."

The bat shifted a little on the perch but otherwise did not respond. Raffa grinned. Echo was feigning sleep, and Raffa knew him well enough not to be fooled.

"Please, Echo? I just need your help to get to the cabin. Then you can go back to sleep, and I won't bother you again the whole day."

Still no response.

"I'll catch you a beetle tonight. Or a spider."

Echo opened his eyes. "Beetle," he said.

"Okay, a beetle."

"Two. *Big* two."

Raffa laughed. "Two big beetles, fair enough. The house is that way, toward daybirth. Just circle it once and come back."

Echo returned in due time. "Man one. Woman one," he said.

"My parents, Echo? You remember my parents, right?"

"Not Da. Not Mam. House no house."

Echo seemed to be talking wobbledywump. Raffa tried to make sense of the bat's report. "Guards, Echo? Like in Gilden—the humans at the Garrison?"

"Guards! Raffa good!"

At least that much was clear. Raffa had to slip into the cabin without the guards noticing. He planned a route in his head. He'd go through the garden, so he could duck between the waist-high terraced beds to stay out of sight. It boosted his confidence to know the landscape so well, in sharp contrast to his wanderings of the past months.

The garden backed onto a slight rise that blocked the cabin from view. Raffa crept up the rise, then waited as Echo flew off again and returned to report that the guards were together in the lane at the front.

"Echo good," Raffa said, his voice low. "Tell me if they start to come this way."

He dashed to the nearest terraced bed and dropped down behind it. Then he crawled to the corner so he could take a peek.

A shock wave jolted him.

House no house.

A blackened, charred pile.

The cabin was burned to the ground.

Trembling, Raffa drew back and almost collapsed against the stone wall of the bed. His stomach rumbled ominously; he held his breath to keep from getting sick.

When had it happened? How had the fire started? And most important, where were Da and Mam? Where would they have gone when they fled the fire? He flatly refused to countenance any outcome other than their escape.

The only home he had ever known.

Gone.

It wasn't possible.

Images streamed through Raffa's mind. The main room, with its big, solid worktable and benches. The fireplace flanked by two chairs and Raffa's stool. The sleeping alcoves: the big one for his parents, across from his own corner pallet. The nicks on either side of the back-door frame, measuring his growth and also Garith's, Garith always the taller.

The utensils and implements for apothecary work, each with its place on a pegged board, so familiar that he could tell at a glance when one was missing. Herbs drying in bunches, hung from the ceiling. The small mirror on the shelf by the door, his reflection wavy in its warped glass.

The cabin had been a place of work and sleep, laughter and arguments, mealtimes and play. There was nothing special about it—except that it was his.

With those memories so real upon solid, Raffa had to peer around the edge of the bed once more, as if the house might suddenly reappear. But the black heap was still there, and he lost his breath again.

The ruins were no longer smoldering, although the smell of smoke still tainted the air. A few days ago at most, then.

I should go through the rubble, he thought, and wondered if he could face seeing the damage and destruction up close.

The decision was taken away from him. Echo landed on his sleeve.

"Guards come," Echo said. He flitted to the perch necklace.

Raffa forced himself to his feet and staggered into the woods.

CHAPTER THIRTEEN

GET to Gilden. Find Mam and Da. Destroy the vine stock. Cure and free the animals.

Those phrases repeated themselves in his head until they had no meaning; they were but the rhythm to which he moved his feet. He walked for hours, well into darkness. The next morning he awoke before daybirth to find himself lying beneath a tree trunk that was partly propped up by a boulder.

Later, he would remember almost nothing of that part of the journey, and would realize that he had been in a state of shock, his body numb, his mind all but empty. If it hadn't been for Echo, he wouldn't have thought to eat. Returning to the perch after his night of hunting, Echo spoke in what for him was a firm voice.

"Raffa no good. Eat."

The bat was right. Raffa found some dried apple slices in Haddie's packet. They brought a little strength and feeling back to his limbs as he ate them on his way to the ferry landing.

The traffic grew heavier the closer he got to the landing. Soon the road opened out to the landing area. Mounted on a stout wooden post at the side of the road was a large placard.

On the placard were three drawings: his own likeness and those of Kuma and Garith!

MISSING, the sign read. IF FOUND OR SIGHTED, REPORT TO GUARDS.

Raffa gasped. He stepped to the side of the road and pulled his hood further forward. His pulse pounding, he glanced around wildly to see if anyone was staring at him. How long would it take for someone to realize that it was *his* face on the placard?

He found himself wishing there were such a thing as an infusion for invisibility—and was instantly disgusted with himself. That he, a serious apothecary, could even think such a thing. It was the worst kind of yearning!

But the thought gave him an idea so rash that he began moving before he could change his mind. He walked *straight up to the placard* and leaned against the post, as if he were waiting for someone. The drawing of his face was right above him!

Raffa hoped with all his might that the ploy would work: Surely no one would expect a fugitive to stand under his very likeness.

He fiddled with the rope coil across his chest, keeping his head down as long as he could before looking up. The ferry landing was busy. People hurried past in both directions, intent on their own affairs. No one paid him the least bit of attention.

Visible, but not seen—it was almost as good as being *in*visible!

But he couldn't stay there long. The wagon traffic had come to a halt. He saw four wagons in a line, awaiting their turn to board the ferry, which would take them across one at a time. The driver of the first wagon climbed down from the seat and walked to the fare collector's hut to pay for his passage. Then he returned to the wagon and drove onto the ferry.

At that moment, Raffa inhaled a dreadful stench. It was coming from the fourth wagon, whose open bed was full of compost. The compost was probably a delivery for the Commons gardeners, who needed a lot of it to grow flowers, fruits, and vegetables for the Commoners.

The last time Raffa had smelled something that strong was when he had been enveloped by Roo after nearly drowning in the Everwide. Could a bad smell help save him again?

Raffa had a hollow reed in his rucksack. Missum Yuli had given it to him at the settlement, to use as a dropper for his apothecary work. He took it out and tucked it into the pocket of his tunic.

He waited until the compost wagon was second in line. Then he sauntered forward and bent down to examine the wagon's rear wheel, as if he were the driver's helper. His legs were shaking so hard that he had to clench his jaw to keep his teeth from rattling.

The wagon rolled forward slowly; Raffa scooted along with it, keeping low to the ground. From that perspective, he could look underneath the wagon, and he saw a pair of boots hit the ground when the driver jumped down to pay his fare.

Quickly Raffa stepped onto the hub of the wheel and in one motion rolled up and over the edge of the wagon bed, landing right on the compost. He sank down into the stinking mass, then lay on his back and pulled at his neckline to make sure the sleeping Echo had breathing room. Taking the reed from his pocket, he stuck it in his mouth and buried himself with handfuls of the disgusting compost—including his face. He was careful to sprinkle only a little compost on the bump that was Echo.

He angled the reed downward, so only the very end stuck out and would hopefully not be noticeable. His heart racing, he struggled to breathe through the reed.

He wasn't getting enough air, and even breathing through his mouth, he was nearly gagging from the smell. The stench seemed almost solid. . . . Was it possible that the bad smell was blocking the good air from getting to his lungs?

It took every shred of his resolve not to sit up and yank the reed from his mouth. This would never do. He had to relax somehow.

Then he heard a little squeak, muffled by his tunic.

"Very smell," Echo said sleepily.

"Shussss," Raffa hissed through the tube—then swallowed a giggle.

Echo had done it again: made him feel better when he needed it most.

* * *

Raffa was astounded by how slowly time crawled when he had to think about every breath he took. He tried to distract himself with the knowledge that it could have been far worse: He was lying down, fully stretched out, and the compost could almost be called comfortable, if it weren't for the smell.

When the wagon began moving, he realized with dismay that only moments had passed. The wheels bumped up onto the ferry; Raffa could feel movement of the water below. Then one of the oarsmen called out to his partner, and the ferry began its journey across the Everwide.

Get to Gilden. Find Mam and Da. . . .

For the first time since he had seen the ruin of his home, Raffa allowed himself to wonder what he would do if he got to Gilden and his parents weren't there. His body went cold—as cold as it had ever been in the Suddens. He shivered to the depths of his bones and began gasping for air again.

No! They couldn't be dead. They'd escaped the fire, they'd gotten away—because if they were dead, wouldn't he know it somehow? Wouldn't he have felt their utter absence when he was there at the remains of the house?

He was sure that he would have. Or maybe he was

just hoping so hard that it felt like certainty.

But if they escaped, why weren't they there, cleaning up, rebuilding?

He shoved away that thought as hard as he could.

The ferry dipped and swayed, bringing his attention back to the present. He frowned. Something about the crossing was bothering him. What was it? He was on his way to Gilden; surely it was cause for celebration that he had gotten this far undetected—

The guards!

He had seen no guards at the ferry landing. No one searching for him, no one checking the wagons.

Then he realized why: Because the guards were on the other side.

They didn't need to be on both sides of the river. On the Gilden side, they could check travelers going either way, and were much closer to both the barracks and the Garrison. Once the ferry docked, they would inspect the wagon, and he would be discovered. . . .

Raffa tried to stay calm. He debated plan after plan: Should he get out of the wagon here on the ferry, and try to slip past the guards as a foot passenger? Should he stay where he was and hope that they wouldn't search the wagon bed? Could he simply bolt and elude them?

No. He couldn't disembark on foot. He'd be too conspicuous, both filthy and stinking, and either the oarsmen or the guards would be sure to notice him. He'd just have to stay where he was, and improvise. For the rest of the crossing, he tried to remember what he could about the landing on the Gilden side.

The wooden dock. Crates, pilings, gulls. A broad path from the dock to the road. A travelers' inn on the left. Maybe he could get out of the wagon without anyone seeing him and then hide behind a piling. But it was sure to be even busier than the other landing; the chances were better than good that someone would spot him.

Raffa heard the lead oarsman call out a hoy. The crossing that had once seemed interminable was ending much too soon. Unable to think of anything else to do, he drew up his legs very slowly, an inch at a time, trying to make himself smaller in the reeking mess.

The wagon rolled off the ferry onto the dock. Raffa heard voices.

"Your name, mannum?"

"Fitzer."

"Fitzer—that's right. Compost for the Commons, is it?"

A guard was querying the driver. Raffa began to

quiver beneath his shroud of compost.

"Yah, and I'm late. Had to wait to cross."

"Won't keep you but a moment."

A double set of footfalls: two guards.

"Go ahead—check the load." The same guard again.

"I checked the last load. It's your turn."

"Where'd you leave your brain? *I* checked the last load. It was barrels of salted pork—"

"The last load of *compost*. A week ago, remember? Not fair for me to have to do it again."

"We take turns checking the load. Doesn't matter what it is. Fair's fair."

"Favor me, Seniors!" The driver's voice again. "Meaning no disrespect, but as I said, I'm already late. Compost, same as last time, same as every time."

A short silence. Raffa could almost see the two guards shrugging at each other.

"Steady," one of them called out. "On your way, then."

The wagon lurched forward. Raffa blew a whoosh of relief through the reed. Saved—by a load of reeking rot!

But he still had to contrive a way to get out of the wagon unseen. After only a few minutes, he felt the wheels slowing. The wagon turned to the left and creaked to a stop.

Raffa heard the driver jump down. A moment later, a metallic squeal sounded, followed by a rush of water. A pump.

We must be in the yard of the inn.

Water glugged and splashed a little longer. Then the man stopped pumping and spoke.

"I don't know who you are, or what you're about," he said. "But I been hauling compost all my life, and I know when my load gains weight along the way. Not much weight, though, so I figure you're just a kiddler."

Raffa was stupefied. The man was talking to *him*. He had known Raffa was there all along!

"I'm going into the inn for a jar of appletip. I don't want to lay eyes on you. The trough is full, and there's no one around. Get out, get washed, and get away before I change my mind."

Raffa heard footfalls receding. A door opened and closed.

He sat up and shook himself like a dog. He brushed off substances he was glad he couldn't name, then scrambled out of the wagon and obeyed every one of the man's orders.

Fitzer, he thought. He didn't even know what the man looked like, but he would do his best to remember the name. As he left the yard, he waved a silent thanks toward the inn.

Then he hurried up the road to Gilden.

The slums were even worse than he remembered. Mud and muck in the streets, grim expressions on every face . . . Raffa supposed he should be thankful that no one met his eye, but he found himself longing for even a nod from people who seemed to have lost the ability to smile.

Raffa caught sight of two guards coming toward him, and he ducked into an alley. Once they had passed, he slipped into the street again. Only a dozen paces later, he saw another guard. He crossed to the other side of the street and bent over, pretending to have dropped something.

The last time he was in the slums, he had seen no guards at all. Why were there so many now? Were they all looking for him? Nerves fraying, he knew that he had to get off the streets as quickly as he could. His plan was to go straight to the house of his friend Trixin; from there, he hoped he would remember the way to the inn she had taken him to before. It had an underground passage where he could hide.

But his first encounter with Trixin, in front of her house, had been wholly by accident, and he had no idea how to get there. As he wandered the slums, constantly on the alert for guards, he came to an unfamiliar square. A crowd was gathered there. Raffa found himself getting almost dizzy, still unaccustomed to being among so many people after the long winter on the mountain with just Kuma and Garith.

People were milling about in obvious excitement. What was happening? In the midst of the crowd, he felt safely hidden, so he paused by a small knot of people to catch his breath. He listened in on their conversation.

"Wheat, I heard."

"Corn, too."

"How much, I wonder?"

Raffa saw a boil on one man's nose, a rash on the neck of a woman. He heard ragged coughing from another woman. Almost without realizing it, he began thinking about the poultices and infusions that could be used to treat them. Yet he knew, too, that the long-term cure was good, solid nourishment, for all three had the sunken eyes of hunger-induced fatigue.

Another woman joined the group. "What's it about, then?" she asked.

"Commoners," one of the men replied, "giving away grain."

"Oh, you're a funny one," the woman said.

"It's true, Larrabel, Chancellor's orders! Two Commoners—see them, across the square there? Hailed everyone, said to bring sacks and line up. Hannik's fetching sacks now."

Raffa knew that for the poor, early spring was the hungriest time of year. Stores of grain from the previous fall would be all but spent, with fields and gardens not yet bearing. But he had never before heard of the Commoners donating food to those in need of it. He thought of Elson and Haddie and the others living at Kuma's settlement, and wondered if the Commoners would be helping those outside Gilden as well.

Then something he had just heard echoed in his mind. *Chancellor's orders.*

The Chancellor had ordered the grain donation?

Raffa shook his head in confusion. For months now, the Chancellor had been the pure essence of villainy to him. He could never have imagined such an act of benevolence from her.

The trained crows infesting the grain at Kuma's settlement with weevils . . . and now the Commoners giving away grain in the slums. Suspicion ruffled his thoughts. Were the two acts related? For all that he reviled the

Chancellor, Raffa knew she had a keen and clever mind. Whatever she did was done with a purpose. If the grain donation was somehow part of her scheme, he needed to find out how it fit.

Scanning the square, Raffa saw a teenage girl walking toward him, her arms wrapped around a sack of grain. She was thin and pale despite her tawny skin, but her dark eyes were bright, which made her look friendlier than anyone else he'd seen so far. He decided to take a chance, and trotted to her side.

"Is that corn?" he asked.

"Wheat!" she said, making the word sound almost like a song.

"Is it true that they're giving it for nothing?"

"True upon truer," she said. "Told my family's name, answered what they asked, and there'll be bread for supper tonight!"

"So what are they asking?"

"Nothing, really. They're doing a census. Where do you live, how many in the family and how old—that's all. Oh, and how long have we lived here."

She cast a quick glance at him; he tensed and turned his head away a little.

"But you have to bring your own sack," she said.

"Better hurry and get one before they change their minds!" She laughed and hurried off.

Raffa faded back to the edge of the square, thoughts buzzing in his head like a swarm of midges.

Until the past winter in the Suddens, he had never known hunger; his parents' work as pothers meant a modest living, but one without need. He remembered his delight over the cattail-pollen bread. What would it be like for bread to be such a rarity *all the time*? He thought of the way the girl had caroled the word *wheat*, the happiness in her eyes, the pallor of her skin.

Then he recalled his time in the Commons, where there was too much food on every table at every meal. And a question began to grow in his mind . . . from the girl, to the crowd of people in the square, to the teeming misery of the slums themselves . . . swelling and spreading until he thought his head might burst from the sheer size and weight of it: *Why were some people wealthy when others were so poor?*

Raffa pinched himself mentally. He couldn't afford the time for contemplation—he had to find the inn. He remembered that it was an inn for Commoners, but for all he knew, there were dozens of such places. How would he ever find it?

No use standing still. He set off back the way he had come; he'd start over, taking different turnings this time.

As he walked, he tried to make sense of what he had learned.

A census? It sounded like the kind of thing the government did every now and then. It also made sense to keep a list of those who received grain, so all families would get a fair share. Maybe everything he had been through was making him see shadows where none had been cast. Maybe the Chancellor—

"Raffa! Raffa, hoy! Raffa, it's me—Jimble!"

Raffa turned and saw a gaggle of kiddlers, too many to count. He recognized the blondest head in the bunch: Jimble, Trixin's younger brother, who had a baby tied to his back and a small girl at each hand.

"Raffa! Remember me?" Jimble shouted.

Raffa's blood turned to ice.

Stop it, Jimble! Stop yelling out my name for the whole world to hear!

CHAPTER FOURTEEN

H E rushed toward Jimble and spoke urgently into the boy's ear.

"Jimble, don't say my name again! No one can know that I'm here!"

Jimble's eyes, blue like Trixin's, lit up with interest. He detached himself and his siblings from the group and bid his friends a cheery good-bye.

"Are they still looking for you?" he asked in a loud whisper as they walked away. "Trixin told me—but that was ages ago!"

"Yes, but I don't have time to tell you everything now. I need to use the underground passages to get to the apothecary quarter. Can you help me?" Before he did anything else, Raffa had to talk to Garith, for two reasons: to see for himself that Garith had returned safely to Gilden, and to find out if Garith knew where Raffa's parents were.

"Sure upon solid!" Jimble grinned. "We'll go by the house first." He gave Raffa the hand of one toddler as if presenting him with a gift. "That's Camma, and this one's Cassa. They're twins, just gone four years. And the baby's Brid. Come, this way—it's not far."

Jimble scooted through the maze of lanes. Camma and Cassa were apparently used to keeping up with him, practically galloping on their short legs. They passed right by another guard, but to Raffa's relief, being in the company of Jimble and his siblings was almost like a disguise: The guard didn't seem to notice any of them.

The lanes began to slope slightly upward, which meant that they were getting closer to the Commons, on the highest ground in Gilden. The slums were giving way to quieter, less crowded streets lined with houses that, while still modest, were in good repair.

Jimble stopped in front of a house Raffa had never seen before, and laughed at Raffa's expression. "I knew you'd be surprised! We've only been here a few days. Wait till I show you!"

Raffa followed Jimble through the door. What a difference from the Marrs' previous home! Before, the whole family had lived in a hovel with but a single, dreary, dirt-floored room. Here, the main room was brighter and more spacious. Raffa saw a table and benches, a kitchen area with a stove and cupboards, and even a few toys scattered on the plank floor.

Pots of herbs lined the window ledges. Raffa recalled that Trixin had grown them at the old house as well. The plants here were growing much more profusely, as if they, too, knew they were in a better place. Bundles of dried herbs hung from the ceiling in one corner, including a wreath of lyptus leaves. Raffa felt a small pang on seeing it: His mother, Salima, tied lyptus sprigs in just the same way.

Jimble chattered without cease. "Da has his own room, Trixin sleeps with Brid, and I have a big alcove in the twins' room. Isn't it grand?"

"Jimble, however did you come by such a house?"

"It's 'cause of Trixin. She done so good working in the pother quarter that the Chancellor organized us this house! And Da has a better job now—he works at the

Commons, night watchman, and does repairs, too."

Jimble was so chattery that it was hard for Raffa to take in everything he was saying. Before Raffa had done a full turn of the room, Jimble had changed Brid's diaper, escorted the twins to the latrine out back, and given them all a drink of water. That reminded Raffa to fill his waterskin, and they were out the door again.

"Trixin probably took you through the Commoners' inn before, did she?" Jimble said. "It's the closest to our old place, but we won't go there. I know a better way."

Several turns and alleys later, Jimble ducked into a shack that looked to be the twin of the Marrs' former home. It had the empty echo and dead air of abandonment. Jimble led the group straight through the house and out the back, where there was a wooden door in the ground.

"Cellar," he explained as he lifted the door.

Steep stairs led down into darkness. Jimble began to descend, but Cassa balked. She hung back, clinging to Camma.

"Dark," Cassa said.

"Dragons in there," Camma said, with absolute certainty.

"Dragons." Cassa nodded in agreement.

Jimble gave Raffa an apologetic look. "They never been in the passages," he said. "Usually when I go down there, it's on my own or with my chummers."

The twins seemed to be on the edge of tears. Jimble snapped his fingers and pointed to the rope across Raffa's chest. "Have a loan of that?" he asked.

Jimble tied one end of the rope around his waist. Then he lined up the twins, wrapped the rope around each of them in turn, and gave the other end to Raffa.

"See now, Camma?" Jimble said. "*We're* the dragon!"

Camma looked before and behind, then giggled. Cassa did the same.

"We're the dragon, we're the dragon!" Camma chanted.

"Roar!" Cassa crowed. Then she pointed at Raffa. "You're the tail."

"I'm glad I'm not the tail. Wag, tail!" Camma shouted gleefully.

Raffa gamely swished the end of the rope while taking a quick, nervous glance around. For someone trying to hide, he seemed to have ended up with the noisiest possible companions.

Jimble's strategy worked: One by one, they climbed down the stairs. Before Raffa descended and closed the door behind him, he picked up a small stone. As the "dragon" began to make its way through the twisting, winding, forking passages, he used the stone to nick a mark on the right-hand wall from time to time, so he could retrace the route without Jimble's help.

He also made a crucial contribution to the twins' happiness by pulling out his lightstick. They were delighted to take turns holding it.

"Is it magic?" Jimble asked, poking a finger at the greenish light.

"Not a bit," Raffa said. "It's made from a kind of fungus that grows in the woods. On dead trees. They glow in the dark, natural."

Jimble blinked, once each for the words *fungus, woods,* and *trees,* then shook his head in wonder. "Shakes and tremors, what a sight that must be!" he exclaimed. Raffa sensed that the forest was as foreign to Jimble as the slums were to him.

"It's a good thing, this rope," Jimble said then. "I don't have to worry about them going off." Meanwhile, baby Brid bounced along on Jimble's back, sucking on a rag wrapped and tied around a piece of carrot. Jimble was small and slight, but he moved as if he had been carrying Brid all his life, which was probably close to true.

All of Brid's life, anyway.

After a walk that was shorter than Raffa had expected, Jimble stopped in front of a rickety wooden ladder. "You climb this, it comes out in another passage," he said. "Only one way you can go, to the left. Then there's a set of steps, and you'll come out of a cellar door like the one we went in. Don't go through the house—it might not be empty. Just jump the wall at the side."

It sounded straightforward enough. "Where will I be then?" Raffa asked.

"Why, at the Commons wall, of course! Didn't you say the pother quarter? That's where you're headed?"

"Yes, but how will I get through the gate?"

"Oh!" Jimble smacked himself on the head. "Sorry. I forgot you wouldn't know. You won't be anywhere near the gate! See, there's no wall there—I mean, there is, but it's just the backs of buildings. And there's a gap between two of them. It's boarded over, but me and my chummers, we pried out the nails, except for the top one, so it swings. You'll have to squeeze through, then between the buildings. That'll be the kitchens, and the pother quarter is off to the left, right?"

Raffa was impressed. Jimble seemed to know his way

around the Commons even better than Trixin.

"I'd take you myself," Jimble went on, "but—"

"That's okay," Raffa said hastily, glancing at the twins. Cassa was waving the lightstick, drawing in the air with it, while Camma waited for her turn. "You can keep the stick, I'll make another."

"It's ours, it's ours!" Camma shouted.

"Thank you, Dragon Tail!" said Cassa.

"His name is—" Jimble started to say, but Raffa cut in quickly.

"Cinders," he said loudly, then cleared his throat. "My name is Cinders." He was worried that if the twins knew his real name, they might blurt it out at the wrong moment.

Jimble tilted his head in puzzlement. "Er, hem . . ."

Raffa gave him a quick wink.

"Oh! Right! Cinders!" Jimble exclaimed, and returned the wink with his mouth wide open.

"Thank you, Dragon Tail Cinders," Cassa corrected herself.

Talking to the twins was a little like talking to Echo, Raffa thought. The bat had been asleep under his tunic all this time, and Raffa meant to leave him there. He shuddered to think how the twins might react on seeing him.

"Jimble, would you give Trixin a message for me? I want to see her. Ask her if she'll meet me here later—sometime around sunfall?"

"I'll make sure she comes," Jimble promised.

Raffa was grateful for Jimble's friendly cooperation. He hesitated a moment, then said, "You keep the rope so you can all get back easier. Give it to Trixin when she comes to meet me." He hated to be without the rope even for a few hours, but Jimble had been so helpful, it was the least Raffa could do by way of thanks. He held out the end of the rope toward Jimble.

Cassa's lip began to tremble. "But now we won't have a tail," she said.

"Of course we will!" Jimble said. "Whoever heard of a dragon without a tail?" He took the end from Raffa, wrapped the rope around her a few more times, then tucked in the end so it hung down behind her. "See?"

Cassa looked down at the tail, her expression dubious.

"Um, that's a much better tail than I was," Raffa said, "because—because—"

"Because you can wag it yourself!" Jimble finished for him.

Her face brightening, Cassa wiggled her bottom. The rope swayed, and she shrieked with laughter.

Raffa saw his chance and climbed the ladder. The last thing he heard from below was Camma yelling, "Jimble, I want to be the tail!"

Jimble's instructions were better than good, and Raffa was soon peering out from between two buildings of the huge kitchen quarter. It was the perfect place for him to slip into the Commons: The people he saw were almost all servients. No Commoners and no guards.

As he headed for the apothecary quarter, he restrained his desire to run. He did his best to imitate the pace of the servients: a rapid and purposeful walk. Soon enough, the glasshouse, where Uncle Ansel grew tropical and fragile plants, came into view—and Raffa gaped in surprise.

Even from a distance, he could see masses of vivid red through the glass. Which meant that the glasshouse was *full* of the scarlet vine! How had Uncle found so much of it?

He must be making the vine infusion by the barrelful, Raffa thought, enough to drug *hundreds* of animals so they could be trained to do the Chancellor's bidding.

Then a thunderclap of realization shook him.

Raffa's plan had been to dose the animals with the

antidote, wait for it to take effect, and then release them. He knew he would have to wait at least a few hours, based on what had happened with the fox. But during that span, if the animals were given the scarlet-vine infusion again, it would simply undo the benefits of the antidote!

Somehow, Raffa had to prevent them from being given the vine infusion. But how? Thousands of clippings . . . barrels full of the infusion . . . *I'll never be able to do it—not even if Kuma were here to help.*

Shoulders slumped with discouragement, he turned into the short lane that led to the glasshouse, and crouched between some bushes. Someone was moving about inside, obscured by a bank of plants.

Raffa craned his neck. *Move—come out from behind there so I can see who you are. . . .*

It seemed to take forever before the figure began to emerge. An arm and a shoulder. Then another wait, long enough for Raffa's foot to fall asleep.

Finally, the person took a few steps and turned so that Raffa had a clear view.

It was Garith!

CHAPTER FIFTEEN

RAFFA wanted to whoop for joy. His relief was laced with admiration: Garith had made the long and difficult journey back to Gilden on his own.

After peering around to make sure no one else was about, Raffa walked up to the glasshouse and stood where Garith would be sure to see him. It was only a few moments before Garith caught sight of him. His eyes widened, and Raffa saw him glance over his shoulder toward the laboratory. Then he looked straight at Raffa and touched his fingertips together in the shape of a triangle—like the roof of a house.

Raffa understood at once. He was to go to the

apartment where Garith and Uncle Ansel lived. It would be empty now, with his uncle at work.

The apartment was a few minutes' walk from the pother quarter. Raffa cut behind some buildings to avoid the main walkways. He entered the courtyard of the apartment and waited there, relieved to be out of sight of the Commons' foot traffic.

When Garith appeared, Raffa took a quick step forward—then stopped. Garith's mouth was set, his eyes hard with an unspoken challenge. Their last encounter came rushing back to Raffa's memory—and he, too, bristled.

"You didn't think I could do it," Garith said.

Raffa smothered a puff of guilt before replying. "I didn't think you *should* do it," he said.

Garith crossed his arms over his chest in a gesture of defiance. "Since when do you get to tell me what to do? You're my cousin, not my senior."

"I wasn't— I didn't—" Raffa floundered, surprised by his thoughts.

Through all the years of their cousinhood, he had followed Garith around. Garith, a year older, charming, carefree, loved by all who knew him. Raffa realized for the first time that Garith had almost never taken advantage of his position as the elder. He might have gotten his way much of the time because of his charm, but not because he was unfair.

It was Raffa who had been unfair—by refusing to consider what Garith might have wanted. But Garith hadn't helped things by becoming so morose and withdrawn.

"I did the best I could," Raffa muttered, looking down at his feet. "I was only trying to help—"

"If you're talking to me, you have to look up," Garith said. "And if you're talking to yourself, you should stop before people start to think you're quake-brained."

"You're the one who's quake-brained!"

Raffa was astonished that those words had slipped out of his mouth. It was the kind of thing he would have said long ago, in another time and place. Back home, where they had teased each other like this all the time.

Garith snorted. "I know you said 'quake-brained,' but it looks like you said 'wake-pained.' I'd rather be wake-pained than quake-brained any day, so there!"

"Wake-pained? What does that even mean?"

The conversation had somehow become ridiculous. Raffa barked out a brief laugh; he couldn't help himself. After a moment, Garith laughed, too, and in the silence

that followed, Raffa felt the tension between them starting to ease.

"Come on," Garith said. "Let's get something to
eat."

Raffa paused for a quick glance around before they
entered the apartment. Garith noticed and said, "Da
is at the compound. Nobody will bother us. And you'll
hear the wagon if he happens to stop by."

Reassured, Raffa went inside. While Garith made
tea, he got bread and cheese from the pantry. They ate
and talked. Garith did most of the talking.

"When I got to the ferry—you saw the placard there,
right?—I told the fare collector that I was turning myself
in," Garith said. "Funny thing was, it's not a very good
likeness on the placard, so he wasn't sure it was me. I
had to convince him!"

Garith explained that as a courtesy to his father, the
Deemers hadn't sentenced him to time in the Garrison
for his role in Roo's escape. But he was now limited to
the apartment and the apothecary quarter, and could go
nowhere else without his father's supervision.

"They're all acting like—like I'm stupid as well as
deaf," Garith said. "Da won't let me do anything but

clean up. I do everything he tells me—I work really hard—but it doesn't seem to matter. I'm not allowed to work with the botanicals."

"That's beyond daft," Raffa said, then added unthinkingly, "You don't need to hear to make a good infusion." Too late he wondered if Garith would take offense.

But Garith was nodding agreement. "I think I could do *better* than I used to," he said. "It's way easier to concentrate. I don't get distracted by noise."

"Shakes! I never thought of it like that," Raffa exclaimed. "Have you told Uncle Ansel?"

"I've tried. He won't listen." A pause. "He kept asking about you. And Kuma, and especially Roo. I—I didn't know what to do at first. But that turned out to be a good thing. He thought I couldn't understand him. He even tried writing things down, but by then I'd made up my mind."

His eyes grew steely. "If I gave in—if I told him what they wanted, where to find Roo—then I'd have made myself deaf for nothing, right? So I didn't tell them anything."

On the one hand, Raffa was relieved to hear this: It

meant that Roo's hiding place was still a secret and that the attack on Kuma's settlement had nothing to do with Garith. But it also meant that the timing of the attack had been part of the Chancellor's plans, which he had to assume were proceeding inexorably.

"Thanks for not telling," Raffa said. Just saying thanks felt thin and flimsy; silently he renewed his vow to work on an antidote for Garith as soon as he possibly could. He added, "Kuma would say thanks, too, if she were here."

The steeliness in Garith's eyes faded and was replaced by obvious distress. He shook his head. "Da thinks he's doing the right thing. He thinks it so much that he can't see anything else. I know he's wrong, but . . . he's my da."

Raffa stared at the tabletop. He felt bad enough about Uncle Ansel himself; it had to be a hundred times worse for Garith. He started to speak, then remembered that he had to raise his head so Garith could see his lips. Garith's words had made him think of the question he had to ask despite dreading the answer.

"Are . . . are my parents here?"

Garith shook his head.

That simple motion made Raffa feel as if his heart

were being cruelly squeezed.

"What is it? What's wrong?" Garith asked.

It was Raffa's turn to shake his head, because for a few moments he couldn't speak. "Our—our cabin," he said, forcing out the words. "It's . . . it was burned down."

"Bird down? What's that?"

"No, *burned*." Raffa tried to sketch a fire in the air with his hands.

Garith's jaw dropped. "When? What happened? We hadn't heard—at least no one told me—"

"I don't know. I was hoping . . . if my parents were here . . ." Tears stung his eyes.

Garith leaned forward. "Wait, listen. They might not have been at the cabin. They came to Gilden right after we left. They've mostly been staying here since then. Da told me that Aunt Salima has been working in the laboratory. He said that sometimes they go home, but usually when they leave, it's to look for you. They left here just before I arrived."

Raffa's head jerked up. "So—so you don't know where they went this time?"

"No. Maybe Da does. They're supposed to be back tomorrow."

Tomorrow. Never had it seemed so far away. How could he bear to wait so long to find out whether his parents were dead or alive? He closed his eyes for a long moment. Mam and Da would never be far from his thoughts . . . but for now, he had to concentrate on other things. The task ahead of him was next to impossible, and besides, working on it would certainly make the time go faster.

"Garith . . . The animals. Do you know what's happening with them?"

Garith's face closed down and he shrugged.

Raffa knew that shrug. He'd seen Garith use it a thousand times. It didn't mean "I don't know." It meant "I'm not saying."

Raffa also knew exactly what to do—which was nothing. He simply stared at his cousin with a look that was half plea, half glare.

Garith clicked his tongue. "It's the truth. I don't know anything. I'm *deaf*, remember? Even when they do talk about it, I can't hear anything they say." A pause. "And besides, *I don't want to know.*"

He glared back at Raffa, but only for a moment, then dropped his gaze.

I don't want to know.

Raffa understood what his cousin hadn't said aloud. What Garith wanted was to earn back his father's trust and respect. If Uncle Ansel wasn't worthy of that respect, it would leave Garith with nothing. No wonder he didn't want to know any details of what his father was involved in.

But Raffa needed his help. He had to sway him somehow.

"Kuma's settlement was attacked," Raffa said. "By animals."

"*What?*" Garith almost shouted.

Raffa told him about the foxes and the sheep, the stoats and the chickens. His attempts to imitate the animals by gestures probably would have been funny if the conversation weren't so serious. When he talked about the weevils he made tiny crawling motions with his fingers, then mimicked voracious eating.

"Shakes and tremors," Garith said, his lips pale.

"There are so many animals," Raffa said, spreading his hands wide. "They must be planning something bigger. We have to stop them."

Garith put his hands on his head in a gesture of despair. For what seemed like a long time, he didn't move.

Finally he brought his hands down and put his clenched fists on the tabletop. "Senior Jayney meets with Da almost every day. A little after sunpeak. They talk in the yard outside the laboratory."

Jayney was in charge of training the animals and was surely privy to the Chancellor's plans. Raffa had previously eavesdropped on the two men from a small room off the laboratory's entrance. But that was back when he had the run of the pother quarter.

Now there was no way for him to get into that room without risking his uncle seeing him. He thought of the yard outside the laboratory. There was nowhere to hide; it was a wide-open space.

But before Raffa could voice these doubts, Garith spoke again. "They all think I'm useless," he said, his expression fierce. "We'll see just how useless I am."

CHAPTER SIXTEEN

GARITH returned to the laboratory. Raffa followed a safe distance behind. He circled to the far side of the yard and ducked behind the low stone wall. Peering out cautiously, he saw Garith emerge with a broom. Garith began sweeping, moving toward where the wall opened out into the lane.

Raffa found a chink to look through. A short time later, he heard a wagon in the lane and saw Jayney at the reins. Raffa had seen him only twice before, but he was easy to recognize, with his full beard and sturdy build.

Jayney reined the horse, jumped down from the seat, and called out, "Hoy!"

Uncle Ansel came out of the laboratory. Raffa's breath caught in his throat. It was the first time he had seen his uncle since leaving Gilden.

A tide of sorrow . . . then a surge of anger. Each as strong as the other.

Sorrow, because his beloved uncle had betrayed him by sending the screaming owl to stop him and Kuma from escaping with Roo. Anger, because Uncle Ansel was helping the Chancellor—no, not just helping: Uncle Ansel was *leading* the work of creating infusions to dose the animals.

How could Uncle Ansel be so blind to the Chancellor's evil? He had once told Raffa that her support of apothecary work was providing the opportunity to expand the limits of their art—to experiment and invent and create in ways never before possible. But how much was that kind of potential for achievement worth? Surely not the misery of so many animals and people.

As the two men greeted each other by matching palms, Garith kept sweeping. Step by step and sweep by sweep, he worked his way closer to them. The men took no notice of him, but Raffa knew exactly what his cousin was doing.

He was lip-reading!

The conversation was not a long one. Raffa saw that Jayney appeared stern and unsmiling. Uncle Ansel looked like he was objecting to something; Jayney made a dismissive gesture. Then both men got into the wagon and departed.

Raffa rose from his crouch so Garith could see where he was. Garith looked around, then darted out of the yard to join him.

"The slums," he said, panting. "I'm almost sure they said—send the animals into the slums. To get rid of all the Afters."

For what seemed like an eternity, Raffa couldn't even comprehend what Garith had just said.

Finally his brain started working again. "The Afters? Garith, *I'm* an After, on Da's side! Why?"

"They didn't say why." A pause, a flicker of doubt in Garith's eyes. "But—but they *can't* be talking about people like you and—and your family. They're probably starting with the slums since so many Afters live there."

The slums. Raffa had been in the slums that very morning. The girl he had seen, with the bag of wheat—

"That's why they were asking so many questions!" he exclaimed.

He told Garith about the grain handout, and the questions being asked of the slum dwellers. "They're trying to find out which families are Afters. That has to be it!"

"Jayney said something like 'Not quite ready, but soon.' I believe him—everybody's on edge lately, and Da's been working all hours."

Soon? How soon? *It doesn't matter—as long as it's not today*, Raffa told himself, *because I'm going to free the animals tonight.*

"Listen," he said to Garith. "The scarlet-vine infusion—I need to talk to you about it." He explained that he would be giving the animals an antidote to cure them of their addiction, and that he had to make sure the animals would not be dosed again with the scarlet vine afterward. It was a complicated explanation, requiring a lot of repetition and gestures, but finally Garith seemed to understand everything.

"I have to get rid of all the vine clippings," Raffa said. "Will you help me?"

He saw Garith's brow furrow into worry lines and immediately regretted asking for his help. There was surely a limit to the number of times his cousin could stand being put in the terrible position of choosing between his father and Raffa.

"No," Garith said. "It wouldn't take longer than a blink for anyone to notice if the vine disappears. I have a much better idea."

Raffa's eyes grew wide.

"Da doesn't let me make the infusion anymore," Garith went on, "but I'm the one who takes it out to the yard every day, for Mannum Trubb to pick up. I'll make a cinder. He'll dose the animals with that . . . and no one will ever know the difference."

A cinder. Garith meant that he would make a fake infusion and substitute it for the real one. It was an old family joke: a "cinder" was something both harmless and useless. Cinders the cat, who had once lived in Raffa's home, had been a terrible mouser.

"Better than good—brilliant!" Raffa crowed. He laughed in sudden and utter delight, because he knew it could work: He had used the same "cinder" strategy to help free Roo. But Garith didn't know that; he had come up with the idea on his own.

Raffa held out his hands toward Garith, palms flat and together. Garith clapped his own hands around them, and Raffa could have jigged for joy to see the glint back in his cousin's eyes.

* * *

While Garith began work on the cinder, Raffa made his way back to the underground passage to wait for Trixin. He sat down with his back against the wooden ladder and didn't know he had fallen asleep until someone nudged him awake.

"You should take better care. What if I'd been a guard?"

It was Trixin! He'd know that voice anywhere—impatient, with a sharp edge, and still it made him smile. He rubbed his eyes and stood to greet her.

"The lump's gone," he said.

The last time he had seen Trixin was when she had whacked herself on the head with a board to help him during his escape from Gilden. The blow had been hard enough to raise an immediate lump on her forehead.

"I'll have you know it was *days* before it went down," she said with a sniff.

She had a candle stub in one hand and his rope in a coil over her other arm. As she handed the rope to him, she looked him up and down. "You're a good bit skinnier than when I last saw you," she said. "How did you manage to get here? There are placards with your picture. I've seen at least two of them."

Placards here in Gilden, not just at the ferry landing.

Not good news, but important for him to know.

"Why did you want to see me?" Trixin went on, not waiting for him to answer her question. "I have to get back. I can't trust Jimble to put the little ones to bed. He'll have them up all night."

Raffa didn't reply at once; it was hard to know where to start. "How much do you know about . . . about what they're doing with the animals?"

"Not much," she answered—a little too quickly, he thought. "I'm still working mostly with Senior Vale in the laboratory. I don't go to that—that place very often."

"Did you know they sent foxes and stoats to attack Kuma's settlement?"

Her hand flew to her mouth. "It was *Kuma's*? Is she all right? Where is she?"

Raffa stared at her for the merest instant, then looked down at the ground to cover his surprise. *She knew about the attack. She just didn't know* where.

"Yes, she's fine," he said, then explained about Kuma going off to see to Twig. "But at the settlement there were crows, too. They ruined the grain stores, so now everyone's worried about not having enough to eat. Including Kuma's family, and they have a lot of kids."

Trixin looked stricken. "I didn't know," she whispered.

What else didn't she know? Was she aware that the plot was targeting Afters? It struck Raffa then that he had no idea whether Trixin's family were Afters or not. They lived in the slums, or, rather, they had when he first met her, but not everyone in the slums was an After.

Should he ask? He needed to know . . . didn't he?

Raffa opened his mouth, then closed it again.

It had never mattered to him before. Not just about Trixin but about anyone. What mattered was if they were friendly or kind or funny or a hard worker or any of a hundred other things. Trixin had proved her friendship more than once. She had earned the right to the truth, no matter what her family's background.

"Trixin, they're targeting Afters. That's why they picked Kuma's settlement—because most of the people who live there are Afters. But I think it was sort of a test. What they really want to do is clear out the slums."

Trixin's eyes had narrowed while he was speaking. "Afters! Wherever did you hear such nonsense?"

"Jayney and my uncle were talking, and—and, well, Garith has gotten pretty good at lipreading."

She looked uncertain for a moment, then tossed her head. "I don't believe it for a minute. He must have gotten it wrong. Jayney has a beard like a rat's nest—you can't even see his mouth."

It seemed that she had already made up her mind, and he knew how stubborn she could be. How could he convince her?

"Okay," he said. "Say that maybe we're wrong. . . . Don't you want to know for certain?"

Trixin began pacing up and down the passage. "Jimble says he took you by the house," she said, in what seemed an abrupt change of subject.

"Yes . . . um, it's nice," he replied with a puzzled frown.

"That's right," she snapped. "A *lot* nicer than our old place. And did you know that I'm one of the only tendants given meals from the kitchen? The Chancellor arranged for that! Brid and the twins have milk to drink every day. And my da—he's not a night slopper anymore. . . ." She stopped and turned away.

He understood then what she was saying. She couldn't help him—couldn't risk losing her job, because her family's well-being depended so much on her.

Silence filled the passage. The longer it lasted, the further away Trixin seemed to be moving from him, even though she was standing still.

Finally she turned back and spoke to him without meeting his eyes. "There's something you don't know, something that happened here in the winter. About two months ago. All three of the little ones took ill—the twins and Brid. That's the way it happens, they get ill and then they get better, one after the other."

Although baffled once again, Raffa sensed that what Trixin was saying was important to her, so he waited for her to go on.

"But this time, it was the dread wheezes. I can't even tell you how awful it was. They coughed and coughed and coughed, and then they'd wheeze and croak and gasp for air. A horrible noise . . ." Trixin shuddered at the memory. "Jimble and I were up all hours with them. Da helped during the day, but nights he had to go to work or he'd be dismissed. It got so bad, I thought . . . I thought we might lose Brid."

Raffa recalled his afternoon with Trixin's siblings— all of them hale and healthy. "But they're fine now," he said. It was a question, not a statement.

Trixin looked him in the eye. "Finer than fine," she said. "Thanks to your parents."

"My parents?" Raffa almost screeched in surprise.

She nodded. "Your da made infusions for them. Then he and your mam came and fetched all three of them to the apartment, and nursed them there for nearly a week, so Jimble and I could get some sleep, we were half-sick ourselves. Your mam sat with them for hours over a lyptus-steam basin. I could have bought infusions from the pother stall at the market, but nobody else would've done what they did for us. Camma and Cassa might have gotten better on their own, maybe, but they saved Brid's life, sure upon certain."

The lyptus wreath at Trixin's house—it was *one of Mam's!* Raffa felt a jumble of emotions: relief for Trixin's family, pride in his parents, and the ache of missing them renewed. "I'm glad," he said quietly.

"It's *them* I owe, not you," she said, in her usual blunt matter. "But they wouldn't have been here in Gilden if it weren't for you, which I suppose means that it *is* you, in a way. So here's what I've decided. I don't know what you want me to do, and I don't care."

His heart sank and he started to speak, but she glared at him, as if daring him to interrupt her.

"I'm going to tell you what I *will* do: I'll keep my eyes and ears open, and whatever I find out, I'll let you know somehow."

Spying.

She was offering to become a spy.

"Another thing," she went on, "I don't ever—

ever—want to know what you're doing. Don't breathe even a word of it to me."

Raffa was almost awestruck: She had come up with a way to help while still protecting herself and her family. But he didn't want to think about what would happen if the Chancellor should find out.

"That's fair," he said.

"Fairer than fair."

Raffa held up his hand toward her, to match palms. It was not something he usually did. It was something grown-ups did.

She flattened her hand against his for a solemn moment. Then she used the same hand to rap him on the head once with her knuckles.

"Yow!" he said, rubbing the spot, which really did hurt.

"Try using a board next time," she said, and they both laughed.

The conversation continued, following Trixin's rules. Raffa asked questions without revealing his plans; she answered without asking why he wanted to know.

"How do the animals get fed?"

"Depends on the animal. Which ones?"

He thought a moment. "The foxes. And the stoats."

"All the meat-eaters are fed fish."

"How often?"

"Twice a day, morning and evening."

"The fish come from the river?"

"And the Vast, of course. You're the country lumpkin—don't you know where fish come from?"

"Sorry. What I meant was, How do the fish get to the compound?"

"By wagon. From the northern ferry landing."

"You said evening. Is it sunfall yet?" Here, underground, it was impossible to tell the hour.

"Nearly," Trixin replied.

"So there will be one more feeding today?"

"Yes. In a couple of hours. The wagon makes the delivery, and the animals are fed straightaway. I guess they don't want a big pile of dead fish hanging around the compound for very long."

"Is everything there still the same as before?"

"Since you left? They've built more sheds. And there are four guards on duty now, day and night."

Raffa groaned. *More animals* and *more guards . . . as if things weren't hard enough already.*

Trixin's feet shifted restlessly. "Is there anything else

you need to know? I have to be getting back."

How to do this without getting caught, Raffa thought. But that wasn't something he could ask her.

"I guess not," he said slowly. "I just . . . I wish I knew Gilden better. And I wish Kuma would get here. I don't think I can do this alone. But I can't wait for her, either."

"Hmph," Trixin said. "You should have thought of that before."

Things were adding up far too quickly. The number of guards patrolling the slums. The grain giveaway and census, which seemed to be a way of determining which families were Afters. Garith's discovery that the project's goal was to target the slum dwellers.

Raffa tried to keep panic from boiling up inside him: The attack on the slums could happen any day now.

He couldn't wait for Kuma to arrive. He had to release the animals that very night.

Trixin gave him the candle stub and a few matches. Without a light, she would find her way out by keeping one hand on the passage wall; both she and Jimble knew the turns by heart. Raffa watched her leave, envious of that particular skill.

Get the antidote powder into the food supply. . . . That much he had figured out. He wondered if he could climb into the fish wagon undetected, as he had with the load of compost. He sighed. Compost and dead fish: It was turning out to be a day of bad smells.

But that strategy hadn't even really worked the first time. The driver—Fitzer—had known he was there. Raffa couldn't risk the same thing happening again.

Somehow he would have to be in two or three places at once. He'd have to stop the wagon, distract the driver, and get into the wagon bed.

He sat there for what felt like a long time, unable to come up with a solution.

Finally he couldn't bear to sit still any longer. *I'll have to get back to the ferry landing, so I might as well go there now.* He stood up, equal parts discouraged and determined. Maybe an idea would come to him as he walked.

He began making his way through the passage, thankful for the candle. Even so, it was slow going, his footing unsure in the unsteady light. One hesitant step at a time, he reached what he hoped was the halfway point.

Then he heard footfalls coming toward him. Remembering Trixin's warning about guards, he blew out the candle, flattened himself against the passage wall, and held his breath.

CHAPTER SEVENTEEN

"RAFFA? It's me—it's Jimble."

Raffa exhaled hard. He lit the candle again and saw the gleam of Jimble's blond hair.

"Trixin sent some food for you," Jimble said, holding up a small pail.

Raffa took it from him and pulled out a piece of hard crackerbread. He bit off a corner and softened it in his mouth. It was salty and wheaty and good.

"She said she don't know what you're doing and she don't want to know, either," Jimble went on. "But whatever it is, she said I'm to help you, so long as you don't get me arrested."

Raffa was silent for a moment. Trixin had heard him say that he wished he knew Gilden better and that Kuma were here to help. She had sent Jimble for both reasons. She didn't want to take part herself, for fear of losing her job, but Jimble didn't have a job to lose. Raffa had been right to trust her—she was steady upon solid.

"You do, don't you?" Jimble asked anxiously. "Need my help?"

Raffa nodded. "We have to stop a wagon."

He described his plan in more detail as Jimble led him back through the passage. They made a turn before reaching the entrance they had used earlier in the day.

"This will take us a bit closer to the ferry landing," Jimble explained.

They walked for a while longer, then stopped at a set of stairs so steep it was almost a ladder.

"Wait here," Jimble said, "I won't be long."

He was up the stairs quick as a squirrel, then vanished from sight. True to his word, he was back soon enough, leading a whole pack of children, who all climbed nimbly and silently down into the passage.

Raffa counted seven of them besides Jimble. They looked to be anywhere from about nine years old to fourteen or so, boys and girls, tall and short, thin and stout, the full range of skin colors from freckled-pale to deepest blue-black.

"These here are my chummers," Jimble said to Raffa, keeping his voice low. "You don't need to know their names, and they don't need to know yours."

Jimble was clearly relishing the intrigue, and Raffa could hear a trace of Trixin's bluntness in his voice.

Then Jimble turned to his friends. "Ears, everyone, and Raffa will tell you—"

"I thought we weren't to know his name!" one of the girls exclaimed in a loud whisper. The whole group tittered, and Jimble's face went scarlet.

Raffa stepped forward quickly. "It's okay, Jimble. It's better they know who I am so they know what they're getting into. I'm Raffa, and the guards are looking for me. If you help me, you could end up in a good tremor of trouble yourself. Anyone wants to leave now, go ahead and nothing against you."

He waited a moment. Nobody moved.

"Name's Davvis," said a tall dark boy. "Jimble says you need our help, that's enough for us."

The others all introduced themselves. After Raffa explained what needed to be done, a lively discussion followed; the group seemed expert at conversing in whispers. Raffa wondered whether he was doing the right thing, putting his faith in those he didn't know. His expression must have given him away, for Jimble caught his eye and gave him a quick wink.

As the talk continued, Jimble leaned toward Raffa and said, "Every one of us knows the others, back to front. We might seem all raggedy-taggle, but you'll see how good we do together."

Looking at the faces around him, Raffa saw nothing but concentration and interest. If enthusiasm could guarantee success, he thought, there was nothing this group couldn't do.

Raffa lurked beside the road between the northern ferry landing and the slums. He was torn between regret and relief that he himself would not have an active part in the plan; everyone had agreed that it would be best for him to stay out of sight as much as possible.

Jimble and his friends were posted at various points along the roadside. Raffa waited, all twitch and jitter. To calm himself, he took out the perch necklace and stroked Echo awake.

The sun had nearly fallen; it was the bat's feeding time. Raffa watched Echo swoop about for a few moments. Then Echo flew back to him and landed on his sleeve. In the bat's mouth was a large half-eaten insect.

Echo clicked, and dropped the bug into Raffa's hand. "What—" he started to say.

"Moonwing!" Echo squeaked triumphantly.

"Truly?" Raffa examined the bug; it was some kind of moth, with dark wings and pale crescent-shaped markings that did indeed look like little moons.

Echo made a chittering noise. Raffa could have sworn he was laughing.

"Okay, Echo," he said, shaking his head and smiling. "Moonwing."

Echo ate the moth with relish. "Tasty," he said happily, and flew off again.

Then Raffa remembered a promise he'd made and not yet kept. He spent the next several minutes searching the ground in the fading light, glad to have something to do other than wait. He found not two but three good-sized beetles and tucked them in the pocket of his tunic.

A sharp whistle sliced through the air: the signal from one of Jimble's chummers that the wagon was approaching. Raffa drew back a little farther away from the road, every one of his muscles taut. He realized then that he would far rather endure the stress of action than the helpless anxiety of watching.

Jimble darted into the road several yards in front of the wagon, then tripped and fell.

All according to plan.

"My leg, my leg!" Jimble screeched.

The driver jerked the horse to a halt and jumped down from the seat. She hurried to crouch beside Jimble in the road.

"Oh, shake it all!" the driver exclaimed at the sight of the blood dripping down Jimble's leg. The blood was real . . . and fake at the same time: Jimble had borrowed Raffa's penknife and nicked his knee in advance.

Now he was wailing his head off.

"We need to get you off the road," the driver said. She grabbed him under the armpits and began dragging him to the verge.

With the driver distracted, one of the smaller of Jimble's chummers scurried to the back of the wagon and lowered its tailgate. Two others moved into position, armed with botanica supplied by Raffa: burstbean pods and lumen husks. The pods would explode noisily while the lumen husks emitted flashes of phosphorescence. Their purpose was to startle the horse. When it reared, the wagon would be jerked and tossed. With the tailgate lowered, the load of fish would spill onto the road, ready for the next step.

The two chummers began throwing a barrage of pods and husks against the wagon wheels.

POP! POP! CRACK! FLASH!

But the horse was old and well-trained. It did nothing more than stamp its feet and snort at the disturbance.

The wagon didn't budge.

More pods and husks were thrown with the same result, except for one thing: This time, the driver noticed. "What in the name of the Quake—?" She started to stand up.

"No, no!" Jimble shrieked. "Don't go! Don't leave me!" He clutched at the driver's leg.

As Raffa watched in helpless alarm, he was furious—with himself. His instincts had been sound: He should never have trusted such an important task to a bunch of kids he didn't know. He realized that he wasn't being entirely fair: Jimble's friends had performed their assignments perfectly. The horse's stolidness was hardly their fault.

But Raffa pushed that thought behind his utter dismay. Now he would have to wait until tomorrow evening for another attempt. And it wasn't just the wagon.

Garith would have to risk making a second cinder as well. . . . And what if the Chancellor launched her next attack during the day?

A sudden moment of silence: Jimble stopped wailing to take a breath. Raffa saw a look pass between him and Davvis, who was loitering near the wagon. Then Jimble began screaming even louder.

"I'm dying, I'm dying! My leg, it's going to fall off!"

"Don't be ridiculous," the driver said, raising her voice above Jimble's screams. She crouched again to examine his leg. "It's barely more than a scratch—"

Meanwhile, Davvis had crept up to the horse. Raffa couldn't see what Davvis was doing, but whatever it was, the horse responded at once.

It gave a high whinny that sounded almost like a laugh, then pranced forward a few steps as Davvis leapt out of the way of its rear hoofs. The wagon jerked and lurched—and, at last, the huge pile of fish poured out onto the road.

Raffa wanted to jump and clap and cheer. They had done it! And he was glad none of them could see his face reddening in guilt over his momentary loss of faith.

"Whoa now, steady!" the driver cried out as she leapt to her feet and grabbed the horse's bridle. Her efforts were considerably hampered by Jimble, who clung to one of her arms.

"Don't worry, Missum!" called a sweet-faced girl with a crooked front tooth. "We'll get it all loaded up for you!"

The boys and girls swarmed the wagon and began reloading it. Each of them had a pocketful of the antidote powder, which they surreptitiously scattered on the fish. The fish were wet and slimy; the powder clung, and most of it dissolved quickly into invisibility.

It didn't take long for Jimble's friends to finish. By the time they were done, all of them were coated with fish slime and glittery with loose scales. Raffa was glad they were too far away for him to smell.

"All steady, Missum!" the girl reported. Jimble's wails had subsided to very realistic sobs. He stood and limped a few steps as his friends gathered around him.

"These your chummers?" the driver said. "They're a good lot. You take care upon caution now—no more running out into the road, hear?"

She flipped a coin at Jimble, whose leg seemed to have made a miraculous recovery: He jumped in the air to catch it.

As Jimble and his friends watched the wagon roll

down the road, Raffa hurried to join them. He tried to express his thanks, but they waved aside his words.

"No need for thanks."

"Good fun, that was."

Except for Jimble, they all stank of fish, but somehow it didn't smell so bad when everyone, including Raffa, was grinning broadly. He turned to Davvis. "What did you do to the horse?"

"Oh, that," Davvis said. "Gave him a little tickle to his—you know, his underparts. Just enough to make him jump."

Everyone laughed and began clapping one another's hands in satisfaction. Then Jimble gave a whoop and held the coin aloft.

"Market tomorrow, everyone! This'll buy comb honey for all of us!"

CHAPTER EIGHTEEN

IT was nearly dark now. Jimble's friends scattered; Raffa and Jimble headed back toward the underground passage. Along the way, Echo flew to Raffa's sleeve.

"Ouch!"

Jimble turned in surprise.

Raffa lowered his arm to his side, hiding the bat. "Ouch!" he said hastily. "I, er, turned my ankle. I'll be okay." He stood on one leg and shook the other in what he hoped was a convincing manner.

"You sounded funny," Jimble said. "Sorta squeaky-like."

Raffa cleared his throat and squeaked, "You mean like this? I was just, um, surprised, I guess."

Jimble giggled. Raffa was relieved that the moment seemed to have passed. He would have to remind Echo about not speaking in front of other people.

"What Davvis done—that was quick thinking, wasn't it?" Jimble began to rehash their successful mission.

"You were brilliant, too," Raffa said. "You fooled that driver through and through."

Jimble looked so pleased that his grin nearly split his face in half.

That's one thing seen to, Raffa thought. He could only hope that Garith had succeeded with the cinder. The animals wouldn't be dosed again with the vine infusion until morning, so Raffa would have the night to free them.

Jimble spoke as if hearing Raffa's thoughts. "What's next?" he asked, his face alight with eagerness.

Raffa understood all too well how difficult his next task would be; it would be beyond helpful to have Jimble with him. He started to speak, then stopped.

It was one thing for Jimble and his friends to help with the wagon. That had been out in the open, on the road, the nearest guards at the ferry landing well out of sight. If by some stroke of bad luck, the guards had happened on the scene with the load of fish scattered in the road, it would have looked like an accident.

By contrast, the shed compound was isolated, forbidden, heavily guarded. There was no way Jimble's presence could be explained away if he was caught there with Raffa—and Raffa would never forgive himself if that happened.

So he looked Jimble in the eye and said, "Nothing more until tomorrow. I can't even see straight, I'm so tired. Will I be all right sleeping here tonight, do you think?"

Jimble's momentary disappointment was allayed by Raffa's last question. "Come!" he said. He led the way down yet another short passage. It dead-ended after a dozen paces. A shallow recess in the rock wall, about knee-high, formed a ledge wide enough to lie down on.

"The guards hardly ever come down here at night," Jimble said, "and if they do you can almost always hear their boots."

"Why do you know so much about the guards?" Raffa asked.

"Oh, we have a bit of fun with them, time to time," Jimble answered. "They don't seem to enjoy it as much as we do." He widened his eyes innocently. "But we don't get into any real trouble. Trixin would skin me alive."

Raffa chuckled. "Now there's a truth if ever I heard one."

Then Jimble frowned. "Been a fair lot of them in the slums lately," he said. "Guards, I mean. Don't know why. It's not like things is any different there these days."

I was right—there *are* more guards in the slums now, Raffa thought. Jimble's observation seemed to confirm Garith's discovery that the slums were indeed the project's next target.

"Do you know anything about the northern slums, Jimble?"

The northern slums were not far from the shed compound, and seemed the likeliest place for him to hide after releasing the animals.

"Not much, but what do you need to know?"

"Just that if I ever end up there, is there somewhere to hide?"

Jimble screwed up his face. "Wish Davvis was here. He knows the passages and all, 'cause he used to live there. Wait—I remember. There's a house all fallen in. . . ."

He proceeded to tell Raffa how to get to the house

from the main road. Raffa repeated the directions, then said, "I'll see you tomorrow. Double thanks for tonight, and tell your friends again, too, will you?"

"I will. Steady sleep to you!" And Jimble scooted off.

Raffa had no plans to sleep, but he needed to eat. He sat on the ledge and rooted through the pail of food Trixin had sent earlier that evening. He ate another piece of crackerbread, a handful of beechnuts, and a few dried plums. As he chewed, he thought about the shed compound and a problem he had not yet solved.

Once he released the animals, he had no way to get them out of the city. If they ran west, as he and Kuma had when they made their escape, they would get to fields and foothills fairly quickly. In any other direction, they would be trapped in Gilden and would surely be either recaptured or killed. Nothing about his task that night would be easy, but this part seemed an impassable obstacle.

Especially on his own.

Sending Jimble home had been the right thing to do, Raffa told himself. He had to repeat it fiercely in his head, to drown out a whisper of regret. And it was less than useless for him to wish for Kuma's appearance. At best, she might be back at the settlement tonight, but

Raffa suspected that she would stay in the gorge for at least a couple of nights, so she could check Twig carefully for any signs of illness.

The candlelight flickered, and Raffa tensed immediately. Was there a draft from someone entering the passage? He blew out the candle and fanned at the air blindly to dissipate the smoke.

He strained his ears for several long moments but heard nothing.

The silence and the darkness began to fill him up inside. His reunion with Garith and the camaraderie of Jimble and his chummers now seemed a faded memory. Underground and alone, Raffa felt as if he had been buried and forgotten.

Tears of self-pity smarted in his eyes. He blinked them away angrily. If only he could talk to his parents about everything! He battled against the thought that they could have perished in the fire, but he couldn't stop the image that filled his mind: a solid wall of flames destroying the cabin—

Raffa sat up straighter. *Fire* . . .

An idea had come to him, vague and formless at first, then rapidly gaining shape and solidity. If it worked, he could cross two crevasses with one leap.

It seemed that the mere thought of his parents was helping him, even without them being there.

He lit the candle again and headed back through the passage to Jimble's loose-board entry to the Commons. From there, he went around the long way, staying in the shadow of the Commons wall, until he reached the back of the stables and the path to the shed compound.

Raffa walked through the scrubland beyond the stables. Soon he felt Echo stirring, and he pulled out the perch necklace. A quick look around: The area was deserted. He took the time for what might well be his last pleasant moment of the night.

"Look, Echo," he said, holding out his hand. On his flat palm were the three beetles he had collected earlier.

"Beetle!" Echo squeaked. "One—two—many!"

He flapped off the perch and circled overhead. Raffa tossed the first beetle into the air; Echo caught it and crunched greedily. The other two beetles went the same way. Raffa grinned to hear Echo's chitter of delight.

But he sobered quickly, his thoughts back to the task. Echo returned to the perch, and they continued through the brush until the fence around the shed compound came into view.

Trixin had said that there were now four guards patrolling the compound at all hours. Crouching in the tall grass, Raffa heard the gate creak open, then saw the light of a bobbing lantern. He watched as one of the guards patrolled the circumference of the fence. After finishing his round, the guard went back inside the compound.

"Echo," Raffa whispered, "you can feed again if you want. But if you see a human coming this way, be sure to tell me, okay? And if I need you, I'll whistle."

Echo chirped in understanding and flew off.

Raffa backtracked until he was well away from the fence. Then he set about gathering tinder: twigs, dead grass, dried leaves. He had amassed a good-sized pile by the time Echo returned, clicking a warning.

Another guard came out of the gate to make his round. In the moonlight, Raffa could see a flash of metal on the man's cap: some sort of insignia, which meant he held a higher rank than the previous guard. Security had indeed been increased since Raffa and Kuma had escaped with Roo.

When the second guard had returned to the compound, Raffa emptied his rucksack and packed it with as much tinder as it would hold. It would probably take him at least two trips; he had to work fast.

He scurried past the gate, which was on the south side of the fence. He began laying a trail of tinder in front of the gate, slanting to the east. Every few paces, he tossed in a few lyptus nuts, which contained a highly flammable oil. It was a scanty trail, but he didn't need a fierce fire. The presence of flames alone should be enough to deter the animals.

He went back for more tinder. His plan called for a second fire, extending from the southwest corner. As the animals came out, they would have to run west to avoid the first set of flames. Then the second set would keep them from turning north.

The fire would also draw the guards outside the fence, leaving the sheds unattended. Two challenges, one solution, a tidy little package—

If it worked.

The air was still, no wind or even a breeze. The ground was muddy, damp, and cold. *Good. That will keep the fire from spreading.*

When he turned the corner on the east side, he was surprised by a new fence forming a small enclosure. He put his eye to a knothole and saw two sheds.

Why two more sheds, completely separated from the others?

Raffa whistled softly for Echo. He sent the bat over the fence to investigate.

Echo returned after only a few moments. "Big," he said.

Big? Had they somehow managed to capture another bear? Or worse, two?

"Big like Roo, Echo?"

"Not bear."

Not a bear. Definitely welcome news.

"One two, one two," Echo said. "Red."

Two in each shed. Four altogether, if Echo's count could be trusted. *Red* . . . "Oh! Foxes, Echo—like Red?" Raffa frowned. Why would they separate four foxes from all the others?

"Not red."

Raffa flapped his hands in frustration. "Red, not red? Which is it, Echo?"

"Not red. Big."

Raffa took a deep breath, held it, blew it out slowly. *Think.*

Echo was describing exactly what he had seen and

sensed in the two sheds. He had said "Red" for a reason. What would remind Echo of a fox and make him say "big" as well?

Raffa gasped in sudden understanding.

Like foxes, but bigger.

The new sheds held wolves!

Now Raffa had yet another problem. Should he release the wolves? If he did, they would panic the smaller animals—to say nothing of the danger to himself. But if he didn't, the Chancellor was surely planning to use them to attack people.

The thought sickened him. He had to lock his knees to keep his legs from trembling.

One thing at a time. He decided to free the animals in the main compound first. Once they were away, he would try to figure out how to release the wolves . . . if he could marshal enough courage.

Near the northeast corner, Raffa found two knot-holes in the boards of the fence. He had prepared his rope in advance, tying a string to one end. After he pushed that end through one of the holes, he sent Echo over the fence to pick up the string. He poked two fingers through the other hole. It took Echo three attempts, but he finally managed to drop the string onto Raffa's fingers.

Raffa pulled the string and the end of the rope came with it. He tied a firm knot and flung the other end over the fence. The rope was looped through the two knot-holes and secured so he could use it to climb out of the compound.

He hurried back to the southwest corner and pulled out a match. "Please please please let this work," he whispered.

CHAPTER NINETEEN

R AFFA lit the tinder and watched to make sure it
ignited. Then he ran as fast as he could to the
gate and set the tinder there alight, too. He dove into the
brush, his heart battering his chest.

It didn't take long for the fire to spread. As he hastily
repacked his rucksack, he could hear the dull bursts of
the lyptus nuts exploding in the heat, their oils feeding
the flames. His muscles coiled tight, he began counting,
aloud but under his breath, to calm himself.

One . . . two . . . three . . . four . . . five—

The gate swung open. The guard coming out to do
his round saw the flames.

"Fire!" he shouted. *"HOY, FIRE!"*

The other three guards came running and began trying to stamp out the flames. In that instant, Raffa saw the flaw in what he had thought was his clever plan: Of course the guards would try to put the fire out! If they succeeded in extinguishing it before he had released all the animals, there would be nothing to stop them from running in all directions.

Which meant that he had even less time than he'd thought.

But the lyptus nuts were helping. As the guards stamped, the nuts exploded under their boots, and the small splatterings of oil reignited the smoldering tinder.

It might still work.

He had to wait until all four guards had moved away from the gate, which seemed to take an eon. Then he dashed toward the compound, staying low to the ground. It was the longest twenty paces of his life: He was fully exposed, should any of the guards look in his direction.

Reaching the gate, he slipped inside and ran to the shed at the far end of the compound. A quick look back: The guards were still outside the fence.

He opened the shed door and stepped inside. It took a moment for his eyes to adjust to the darkness, with the slatted ceiling straining the moonlight. He closed his eyes, counted to five, and opened them wide.

On the shelves were cages full of sinuous weasel-like creatures. *Stoats.* There were so many! Far more than when he had last seen them. He would have to open dozens upon dozens of cages.

A swell of discouragement nearly overwhelmed him. If only he had some help! How could he possibly be expected to fight the Chancellor's power on his own?

But there was at least a kernel of good news as well. The animals he'd seen on his first visit to the compound months earlier had all been dosed into an unnatural state, asleep but twitchy. The stoats he saw now were pacing in their prisons and hissing at him. They appeared to be acting the way wild captive stoats would.

Raffa felt a pulse of cautious optimism. The animals' behavior seemed to indicate that the antidote powder on the fish had worked—and that Garith had succeeded with the cinder.

But he had to make sure. He moved closer to the nearest shelf, peering into the first cage. The stoat inside hissed menacingly and clawed at the bars; Raffa drew back with a jerk. He tried again, but the stoat whirled about and retreated to a far corner of the cage.

Were the stoat's eyes black now? Or did they still have the telltale purple sheen?

Raffa tried other cages, with the same result. *I don't have this kind of time! I have to release them now! But if their eyes are still purple, I can't free them. They won't be themselves—they won't last the night out there!*

He fumbled for a match and lit it. The flare blinded him momentarily. Blinking hard, he held the match close to one of the cages; the stoat half-closed its eyes against the light, and Raffa almost cried out in frustration. He gritted his teeth and stared at the animal as hard as he could.

Black! Its eyes are black!

Before the match burned out, he checked the neighboring stoat's eyes. *Also black.*

No time for cheering. Raffa began unlatching the cage doors, working as fast as he was able. Too fast: He pinched a finger in one of the latches and let out a yelp of pain.

Finally the last stoat was freed, and Raffa followed it out the door. He watched the stream of stoats running through the compound; the first of them had already found the gate. To his relief, he saw them immediately turn west, away from the line of flames.

He listened for a moment longer, fearful that the guards would spot the animals, but apparently the stoats were staying away from the guards as well, for he heard no shouts of alarm.

The next shed held badgers. They were larger animals, with broad white markings that would show up in the moonlight, making it far easier for the guards to spot them. Racked by indecision, Raffa hesitated for precious seconds, then slammed the door and headed for the next shed. The badgers would have to wait; he would release them last.

Third shed. Foxes. By now Raffa had a system. He had found that it was faster to flip down the latches on a whole row of cages, two at a time, using both hands, and then go back to pull them open. He was able to free the foxes in half the time it had taken him to do the stoats, and his spirits rose a little.

As he headed for the fourth shed, a guard hurried in through the gate. Raffa saw him first, but it did him little good. The guard spotted him before he could even react.

"HOY, YOU!"

Where's Echo? Why didn't he warn me?

Raffa turned and fled toward the northeast corner of

the compound. A flood of foxes was running toward the gate. The guard cursed and began dodging the animals as he yelled for his colleagues.

Grabbing the rope, Raffa began half-scrambling, half-climbing the fence. To his alarm, he felt the rope give a little. Had he not tied it tightly enough?

He climbed a step higher—and the rope gave still more. Then he knew: It was being shredded by the glass shards at the top of the fence. Any moment now and it might get cut through completely!

Raffa held on to the rope with one hand and made a desperate grab for the top of the fence with the other. He cried out in pain as glass sliced his palm. He flung his legs over and fell down the other side, barely managing to get his feet under him. Then he hit the ground, and rolled.

Before he had taken another breath, he was crawling back toward the base of the fence to untie the rope, refusing to leave it behind. The rope was slippery as he yanked at the knot: His hand was wet—with blood.

Clenching his fist in the hope of stanching the bleeding, he whistled for Echo, and started running toward the road that led to the northern slums. If any of the guards were pursuing him, he didn't glance back to find out.

Echo rejoined him where the lane met the road.

"Midge midge midge midge skeeto skeeto midge!" the bat said happily.

Raffa stopped in his tracks and spun around to make sure that the guards hadn't followed him. The lane was empty. He should have kept running, but he was too angry.

"*Midge? Skeeto?* Is that all you have to say?"

Raffa had enough of his wits about him to keep his voice down, but there was no mistaking his fury. "*Where were you?* You were supposed to warn me if you saw any humans nearby!"

Hanging from the perch necklace, Echo was quiet.

"Echo, why didn't you click? Don't you realize—I almost got caught!"

The bat blinked once, and gave a small, sad chirp. "Click," he said, "click."

"That's what I'm asking! Why didn't you—"

"Raffa under."

Raffa under? What does that mean?

"Echo not under."

Raffa groaned in complete frustration. Why did talking to Echo have to be such a puzzle? "Under not under . . . *What are you talking about?*"

"Raffa under. Human come. Echo click click click."

Now it was Raffa's turn to blink—in sudden and abashed understanding. "Oh, Echo. Oh, no."

Echo *had* clicked. But Raffa had been inside the shed—*under* the roof, as Echo put it—and hadn't heard him.

How could he have overlooked something so simple? And how could he have been so unfair to Echo? Worst of all, his mission had been the next thing to a disaster: He had managed to empty only two sheds. Two out of *twelve*. The Chancellor still had hundreds of animals at her disposal—including the wolves.

Raffa wanted to shake his own self until his teeth fell out.

"Echo, I—I'm so sorry. I should never have—it was all my fault." He stroked the bat with his good hand.

Echo chirped again. "Raffa need skeeto," he said.

Just like that, the bat had forgiven him. Raffa wanted to smile but couldn't summon the strength. He felt like sitting right down in the road. Instead, he wiped his eyes and forced his legs back into motion. He trudged the first few steps, then began a stumbling trot up the road into the northern slums.

First lane, second alley, third house. Those had been Jimble's instructions.

"A house all fallen in" was putting it mildly; what Raffa found was not much more than a woodpile. But toward the back of the collapsed structure, part of a wall and the ceiling above it remained intact, and he was able to slip behind some boards to hide there. Echo flew to a corner under the eaves and roosted.

Raffa took a long drink from his waterskin. Then he pulled out the candle stub and lit it so he could examine his wounded right hand.

The jagged cut ran from below his middle finger to his wrist. He felt a sharp pinch when he flexed his hand, and guessed that there might be a sliver of glass embedded in the cut. He had no tweezers to remove it; all he could do was pour water on the wound, which stung so much that he cursed. Unable to make a proper poultice, he put two yellowroot leaves on the cut, then bound his hand with a rag. Poorly and awkwardly, using only his left hand.

He covered his face with his good hand, squeezing

his eyes shut against the tears. He had failed, almost completely. Now the Chancellor would doubtless put even more guards at the compound. He had lost his only chance to free the animals without getting caught. His sole forlorn hope was that his efforts would somehow delay any plans for an attack, whether in the slums or elsewhere.

The only thing that saved Raffa from his despair was exhaustion. He slumped against the wall and fell asleep almost at once.

Raffa's eyes flew open: He was jerked into alertness by a noise nearby. Someone was scuffling through the rubble. Whoever it was had been running; he could hear the person panting hard.

In his sleep, he had slid down the wall and was now curled up at its base. A more defenseless position was hard to imagine.

Sunlight filtered through the boards. If he moved, whoever was there might hear him. Maybe it was someone scavenging in the debris—why else would anyone be here? And if he stayed quiet, they would go away. . . .

Then—

"Raffa?"

It was Trixin! *Jimble must have told her where I might be hiding.*

He jumped to his feet and came out from behind the boards. "What are you doing here?"

Trixin was still so out of breath that she couldn't answer at once. Finally she managed to choke out the words.

"Your da," she gasped. "He's been arrested. They think he started a fire."

PART III

CHAPTER TWENTY

RAFFA gaped. He tried to speak, but his lips and his tongue and his voice were tangled in knots by his thoughts.

Da—he's alive! He didn't die in the cabin fire! But . . . arrested?

"He's to be brought before the Deemers this afternoon," Trixin said.

Arrested? Deemers? This afternoon?

Raffa grabbed his rucksack. He took a step and tripped over a chunk of rubble. Trixin managed to grab his arm before he fell.

"Where do you think you're going?" she demanded.

Raffa stared at a point beyond her shoulder, thinking of Bantan at the settlement. He remembered how terrible it felt to be suspected of doing something he hadn't done: the shock and anger at the unfairness and, worst of all, the helplessness at not being able to prove Bantan wrong then and there. It would be far worse for his father, who would face imprisonment in the Garrison if he were found guilty.

I can't let that happen!

"It wasn't him," he rasped, his voice still not working right. "I have to— I'm going to the Commons."

"Shakes and tremors, whatever for?"

"The—the Deemers. Where do they—where—"

"What's the matter with you? The Deemers sit in the Hall of Judgment. Is that what you're asking?"

"Yes. Yes. The Hall, where is it?"

Trixin still had hold of his arm, and she gave it a hard shake. "Are you sleeptalking? You sound like you left your brain a day's walk away! Start making sense or—or I'll slap some into you!"

Raffa blinked a few times, then finally focused on her face. "I'm going to that Hall place," he said, "to see the Deemers. To turn myself in."

"What?"

He took a deep, deep breath. It helped; he felt a little less hysterical now. "Look, you said you don't want to know what I'm doing, so I'm not going to tell you anything. Except to say that the fire—it wasn't my da. I'm not going to let them lock him up for something he didn't do."

He tried to unshamble his thoughts. *When I confess and they arrest me, surely they'll let my parents visit me in the Garrison. And I can tell them everything, and they—they'll know what to do.*

He would be sacrificing his own freedom to stop the Chancellor. It sounded like a very noble thing to do. In fact, he recalled saying something similar to Kuma: how a single life—Twig's—was far less important than the chance to save many.

Then why was he suddenly so afraid?

Meanwhile, Trixin was staring at him. "Faults and fissures!" she said. "At least one of us needs to think steady here. I can see it'll have to be me!"

She looked around, found a sturdy plank, and dragged it over. "Sit," she ordered.

Raffa was surprised to discover that it was a relief

for someone else to be telling him what to do. So he sat. She plopped down next to him and began unwrapping the rag on his hand.

"This will never do," she said critically. "It looks like Camma did it, with Cassa's help."

She rewrapped and retied the binding. It looked and felt much better when she was done, although he could still feel the pinch of the glass sliver. "Thanks," he said.

"Now, then," she said. "It's plain as day that you should at least wait for the verdict. What if he's found innocent? Then you'd have turned yourself in for nothing!"

"But what if they say he's guilty? If I wait, it might be too late—"

"There's more to tell, so just listen, will you? When I got to the laboratory this morning, I saw Garith. He said your parents had arrived at the apartment at daybirth, from . . . from wherever they were. He told them you were back in Gilden, and that he thought you were headed for the shed compound last night."

She glared at him. "Now I've told you that part, I'm going to forget I ever heard it. Anyway, your parents started out straightaway to search for you. But right when they were leaving, the guards came and took your da."

Da and Mam know I'm here! Raffa had to stifle his impulse to run outside and yell for them at the top of his lungs. "My mam—where is she now?"

Trixin shook her head. "I don't know. She wasn't at the laboratory when I left. But I'm sure she'll be at the hearing this afternoon."

"Okay. Okay." Raffa had finally accepted that Trixin was right about one thing: He was dazed upon flummoxed about everything, including what to do next. "What do you think I should do?"

"I told you already. You should wait for the verdict. If your parents weren't in Gilden last night, maybe someone saw them and could testify that it couldn't have been your da. Then it wouldn't have to be you sticking your neck out to get your head chopped off."

She stood up, offered her hand, and pulled him to his feet. She examined him critically.

"Pull up your hood," she said, "and walk like your rucksack is really heavy. I'm going to take you straight through the Commons, to a place I know. . . . You're a servient carrying a load for me—got that? Keep your head down."

Raffa summoned Echo to the perch. They followed Trixin down the road and into the Commons through the back gate. It was midmorning, and people were going about their day. Whenever they passed anyone, Trixin would berate Raffa to maintain the guise of his being a servient.

"Keep up, you lazybones."

"Careful, clumsy lummox!"

"Must you jostle it so?"

For the time being, Raffa was still grateful that she had taken charge. But it did occur to him that she didn't have to enjoy it quite so much.

Trixin led Raffa to a small storeroom in the kitchens area. They stepped inside; she pulled the door closed behind them. A single window in dire need of washing struggled to let in a little light. The room contained shelves holding stacks of beakers, nests of basins, an assortment of odd-sized pots and pans.

"Senior Vale keeps the laboratory in perfect order, he doesn't like any mess about," she said. "We were given this space to store extra equipment. I'm the only one who ever comes here. You'll be safe enough for now."

During their walk, Raffa had made up his mind to follow her advice and wait for the verdict—which meant that he would need to sneak into the hearing. If his father were somehow found guilty, Raffa had to be there on the spot so he could confess the truth.

But how much of the truth? "Has there been talk about—about any animals?" he asked cautiously.

She scowled, the frown-furrow between her eyebrows deepening. "No," she said. "Just a fire, that's all I heard."

Raffa suspected that the Chancellor still wanted to keep the animal project secret. Perhaps there would be no charges against his father regarding the release of the foxes and stoats.

"What can you tell me about hearings?"

"They used to be open. Anyone could go and sit in the gallery," Trixin said. "I was there once, for my da's hearing."

A brief silence. Raffa remembered that Trixin's da had served time in the Garrison, unfairly accused of stealing food from a wealthy household.

Trixin tossed her head as if shaking off that memory. "But they changed the rules this winter. Almost all the hearings are closed now. No audience allowed."

"Are there guards?"

"Two, at the entrance."

How many times would he have to get into a place that was guarded? Raffa wanted to pound the wall in aggravation; he restrained himself only because someone outside might hear.

"I have to go to work," Trixin was saying. "But I'll send Jimble here later."

"With the dragon?" Raffa asked unthinkingly. He meant the little ones—the twins and baby Brid. They were sweet and cute and funny . . . and the last thing he needed today.

Trixin looked startled. "The what?"

Raffa explained.

"That Jimble!" she said. "He's forever giving them daft ideas." She shook her head, but he could see the fondness in her eyes. "No, I'll tell him to get a couple of his chummers to look after them for a bit." A sly grin. "The twins are crazy about Davvis."

Raffa recalled feeling alone and abandoned in the underground passage. He'd been wrong to feel that way: Ever since he'd arrived in Gilden, Trixin and Jimble had been helping him. He looked at her, unable to find the right words.

"What are you looking at me like that for?" Trixin snapped. "Just remember, whatever it is Jimble does with you, if you get him into any real trouble, I'll skin the both of you alive."

She marched off without saying good-bye. Raffa raised his hand in salute until she disappeared from view.

CHAPTER TWENTY-ONE

B Y the time Jimble arrived, Raffa had come up with a plan and made a mental list of the botanica he would need. For the first task, Jimble would have to go to the apothecary quarter and speak with Garith, who could supply various items from the stocks in the laboratory.

The list was a long one, and they had no chalk, so Jimble had to memorize it. Together they made it into a rhyming chant to make it easier to remember.

"Rubus berries, brassy blooms, beetroot juice, and mica plumes . . ."

Raffa was impressed by how quickly Jimble mastered the list.

Then Jimble frowned. "This is your cousin who's deaf, right? He won't hear me sayin' it to him."

"Say it to him normal, like you did just now. He'll be able to read your lips. He might have to ask you to repeat some things, but he'll figure it out."

Jimble looked skeptical but said nothing. Raffa rattled on with more instructions. "Easiest is to wait until Garith goes into the glasshouse, and then show yourself. Make sure he's alone, and don't let my uncle see you. And remember, he won't hear you if you call out and you oughtn't to anyway."

"'Course I won't!" Jimble said, indignant. "But I never met him before, so how'll he know that I'm doing for you?"

Raffa stared, his mouth open. Jimble had made an obvious point—one that Raffa had missed entirely.

He closed his mouth and thought for a moment. Then he untied a section of his leather rope, the part that had been damaged by the glass shards.

"Hold this up when he first sees you," Raffa said. "He'll know it's mine."

Jimble scampered away. While he was gone, Raffa attended to his next task, which was to make a few simple combinations with the botanica in his rucksack. His injured right hand proved to be mostly useless. Irritated at himself, he realized that he should have asked Jimble to fetch tweezers, too, so he could have tried to remove the sliver of glass.

Years earlier, his father had insisted that Raffa learn to use the pestle with either hand. Raffa had grumbled at the time. Now he was thankful, and set about grinding a few dendra leaves with his left hand.

Jimble was back within the hour, flushed and triumphant. "Couldn't have been easier," he said. "Garith—he was out in the yard when I got there, and he went and fetched everything. I was away without another soul knowing! And you were right, he *can* read lips. It's better than brilliant!"

A short pause for breath, then Jimble went on. "I wonder, would he teach me? And my chummers, too? Just think if we could talk to each other without making any noise. There's times when that'd be right handy!"

Raffa couldn't help a smile. "I'm sure you could learn," he said, "but it's not as easy as he makes it look. He's worked really hard on it."

Jimble's eyes widened; he was obviously impressed. "Oh—and he told me to say to you, whatever you're doing that needs all this stuff, he hopes it works and he wishes he could help."

Raffa nodded. "He already has."

He had cleared off space on one of the shelves so he could line up the jars and packets of botanica Garith had sent. Then he chose what he needed to add to the combinations he had just made.

Jimble watched with great interest. "What about all them?" he asked, pointing to several ingredients that Raffa hadn't yet used.

"I'll explain in a bit," Raffa said. He wasn't meaning to be secretive, but he thought it wise to delay disclosing a part of the plan that Jimble might not care for.

Raffa used a reed to suck up a small amount of water from his waterskin. He added a little to the botanicals in his mortar and turned the pestle a few times. He looked up to see Jimble staring.

"Want to turn it?" Raffa asked, holding out the pestle.

Brow furrowed and tongue protruding from the corner of his mouth, Jimble turned with such vigor that the mixture was in danger of being sloshed out of the mortar. After only a minute or so, he stopped and stretched out his fingers. "Harder than it looks!" he said.

Raffa raised his eyebrows in surprise. Turning the pestle was something he had begun doing almost before he could walk; he couldn't remember a time when he had found it difficult. He took the pestle again and began turning it steadily, rhythmically, applying more pressure to rougher parts of the paste, speeding up or slowing down, as his experience and instinct decreed. Jimble followed every move with his eyes.

Soon, a smooth, tranquil feeling suffused Raffa's mind, which told him that the combination was ready. He poured it into a jar, then cleaned out the mortar and filled it with another combination.

He let Jimble perform the next steps: adding dried mirberries; stirring in a few drops of water; turning the pestle. It was hard to say who was having more fun: Jimble, being introduced to apothecary, or Raffa, making the introduction. Raffa had never before experienced the satisfaction of teaching someone else a little about the art he loved so well.

He wondered how apothecaries could tell whether a young person had talent. Certainly Jimble was showing both interest and enthusiasm. Was that where talent began?

When the combinations were finished, Raffa took a moment to go over the plan again in his head. It was, he thought, a good plan, not too complicated, but he found himself wishing for one more facet that might bolster its chance of success.

"What's the matter?" Jimble asked.

Raffa pointed at the jar holding the first combination, which included the dendra leaves. "I need a disguise to get past the guards, right? When I take that, it will make my face swell up. But I wish there were a way to make me look even more different."

Jimble inspected him in the light from the window. "How about cutting your hair?"

Raffa's hair was dark and curly and untidy, even when well combed. Over his sojourn in the Suddens, it had grown into a tangle that nearly reached his shoulders. He thought of his likeness on the placard at the ferry landing, which had clearly depicted his curls.

He shook his head. "It's a good idea, Jimble, but I don't have any scissors."

"Use your knife, couldn't I?"

The activity that followed was quite noisy.

"Careful—that's my ear."

"I *am* being careful."

"Yow! Don't pull so hard!"

"I have to saw at it like this. You ought to keep the blade sharpened better."

"*Ouch!* This was a terrible idea. I can't stand it anymore!"

"We can't stop now. It's only half done, you look daft upon foolish!"

"Careful! You almost got my eye!"

By the time Jimble pronounced the job finished, Raffa's whole scalp was smarting and stinging. He rubbed his hand over his head. In some places his scalp was almost bare; in others, patches of matted hair remained. He concluded that the lack of a mirror or glass in which to check his reflection was probably a blessing.

Jimble inspected his work. "It's a bit uneven," he conceded. "I could try—"

"No, thanks!" Raffa said as he snatched the knife out of Jimble's hand.

"Well, anyway, you do look different now."

Raffa nodded in resignation. "Once my face is all swollen, maybe people will think I have some kind of—of disease that made my hair fall out." It seemed the best he could hope for.

He paused for a moment, then spoke slowly. "Jimble, do you remember when we first met? You asked me to show you some pother magic. What we're going to do isn't exactly magic . . . but maybe you could say it's *magical*."

Jimble hopped up and down in excitement. "And we're going to use the pother stuff we just made, right?"

"Yes." Another pause. "I could do this without you. It would be better if I had your help, but you can say no—"

Jimble looked astonished. "Why would I say no?"

"Because it . . . it's going to make you sick."

"No worries there! I don't get sick, not hardly ever. Davvis once dared me to eat a cockroach, and I done it without a blink. I hate getting sick." A shudder. "It was easier just to keep it down."

Raffa sighed. "No, you don't understand. That combination you helped make? You'd have to drink it, *and it will make you sick*. On purpose."

"Oh." The light in Jimble's eyes dimmed. "Oh, shakes. Do I have to?"

"No." Raffa spoke firmly even as his heart sank. "Like I said, I might be able to do this on my own."

"But it would be better if I helped."

Raffa did not reply.

Jimble was uncharacteristically quiet. Then he said, "I'm not sayin' yes yet. I want you to tell me more—what it does and all."

Raffa couldn't help a small smile of admiration. It was the right question. Jimble was every bit as sharp as his sister.

"We put in those mirberries," Raffa began.

"Three of them."

"Right. They're an emetic."

"What's a—a nemmetick?"

"Emetic. It's a combination that makes people throw up. We use it when someone has eaten something they shouldn't. Maybe a little kiddler eats sumac berries—they're poisonous—so we get them to drink this."

"Oh! So it's something you use a lot?"

"Not that often. But I've made this combination before, at least a few times, for my parents to give to patients."

"And it's safe."

"Yes. The infusion we made is a weak one, and I'll only give you a sup or two. And I made another combination for stomach-soothing. You could take that afterwards if you don't feel well."

Jimble scratched his chin. "If Trixin was here, what d'you think she'd say?"

Raffa thought for a moment. Trixin had hit herself on the head with a board that time . . . but he suspected that she might feel differently about potential harm to her younger brother. He honestly didn't know, and was about to say so when Jimble spoke again.

"No, I got to make up my own mind about this." He scowled fiercely. "I so hate it! Your stomach all rumble-tumble—and how it burns your throat coming up, and—and that awful taste in your mouth even if you spit a hundred times—"

Everything Jimble had said was true. It *was* dreadful, there was no way to honey-drip it. Raffa resigned himself to a solo venture. He had no choice but to hope that the disguise would be enough.

Jimble looked up, his blue eyes steely. "You know something else about getting sick? You always feel better after. . . . And you say it's safe, and Trixin says to help you, so—so I'll do it."

"Wait—what?"

"I said I'll do it." Jimble's sunny grin returned. "And what a story I'll have to tell my chummers!"

I wish I had some way to thank him, thought Raffa.

There was nothing in his rucksack that would make a suitable gift. He couldn't give up his knife or his rope or his mortar and pestle. But Jimble was trusting Raffa with his very health; he deserved something in return.

He deserves to be trusted back.

"Jimble, can you keep a secret?"

"'Course I can!"

"No, I mean *really* keep it. You can't tell your chummers. Or the twins. Or even baby Brid."

Jimble giggled, then sobered quickly. "Not my chummers, hmm . . . Not even Trixin?"

"She already knows."

"So it's okay to talk about it with her?"

Raffa nodded. "Yes. But only if no one else is around."

"This must be a quake of a secret!"

Raffa pulled out the perch necklace with a sleeping Echo.

Jimble stared in surprise. "Is it real? And you carry it with you all the time? Um . . . good fun, that."

After the gravity of Raffa's cautions, Jimble was clearly a little disappointed in the "secret."

"His name is Echo."

The bat was not usually awake at this hour, and he

could be grumpy at such times. Raffa hoped that the storeroom's dim light would help put Echo in good humor. He blew on the bat's whiskers. Echo stretched his wings, opened his eyes, and looked around.

"Echo, this is Jimble," Raffa said. "He's a friend, so it's okay."

"Jimble friend," Echo said.

Jimble shook his head and poked a finger at one of his ears. "Did you hear that?" he said doubtfully.

Raffa grinned. "Hear what?" he teased.

"Hear what?" Echo chirped. "Jimble friend."

Jimble gawped, his eyes and his mouth perfect circles. "Wobble me . . . ," he whispered.

Then, with his arms outspread, he spun around twice and fell to the ground, landing on his back. "Wobble wobble WOBBLE!"

Laughing, Raffa pulled him to a sitting position. "Hold out your finger," he said.

Jimble obediently extended his forefinger, and Echo fluttered to hang there. With the tiny creature dangling before him, Jimble was so still that he seemed to have stopped breathing.

"Jimble friend, Jimble good," Echo said.

"That's right, Echo," Raffa replied.

Then he sat back and watched as Jimble and Echo got to know each other. Never in his life had he seen anything quite as delightful as the wonder in Jimble's eyes.

After some debate with himself, Raffa decided to leave Echo in the storeroom. As much as he hated being separated from the bat, there would likely be a lot of people at the Hall of Judgment. He didn't want to risk anyone hearing Echo speak.

"Echo," he said, "I'll meet you here later, okay?" He hesitated for a moment, then continued, "If it's after dark, you can go out and feed, but come back when you're done." Echo could get into or out of almost any structure made by humans. Even the solidest of buildings had cracks a tiny bat could slip through.

Echo blinked a few times, chittered once, then flew to a dark corner to roost. Raffa could no longer deny that Echo's eyes were now nearly black. Only a tinge of purple remained. Could the bat be reverting to his natural state?

I can't worry about it now. I'll think about it . . . later.

With their preparations complete, Raffa and Jimble slipped out of the storeroom and walked to the Hall. Raffa's face was swollen grotesquely. His cheeks and jowls puffed out; his eyes were barely more than slits. The hack-and-saw haircut was literally the crowning touch. At close range, anyone who knew him would recognize him, but he now bore little resemblance to the likeness on the placards.

The last time Raffa had been in disguise was when he and Trixin and Kuma entered the Commons gate dressed as supposed denizens of the Forest of Wonders. With a grim inward chuckle, he realized that he had been far more nervous then, because it had been his first attempt ever at using a disguise. And they had succeeded.

So I should be feeling more confident this time. No, he corrected himself, *I am feeling more confident. I am!*

Maybe saying it loud enough in his mind would make him believe it.

They joined a short line of people who had business in the Hall. Raffa could see the two guards at the entrance stopping each person and querying them.

Raffa was sweating and his face was almost unbearably itchy. He wasn't sure whether it was anxiety or the infusion—dendra leaves caused swelling, and sometimes itching too. When only two people remained in front of them, he nudged Jimble, who took a small apothecary jar out of his pocket. Jimble stared at the jar for a long moment, then took a deep breath and downed its contents in a single gulp.

A few moments later, they were nearly at the entrance. Jimble groaned and clutched his stomach.

"I—I—I don't feel very well," he said in a loud voice. "I think—I might—oh, no—"

He staggered forward, stopping between the two guards. With another groan, he turned until he was facing the line. He let out the loudest, longest burp Raffa had ever heard, and it was followed by the inevitable.

Jimble began to vomit.

Spectacularly.

A stream of brilliant colors spewed from his mouth. It looked for all the world like he was puking up a rainbow!

The guards and those at the front of the line backed off a step, but no one could tear their eyes away.

"Ewwww!"

"Oooooh!"

"Disgusting!"

"Amazing!"

"The green—it's so shiny!"

"Purple! Wait, now it's yellow!"

On their way to the Hall, Raffa had fed Jimble an array of bright-hued botanicals. Some were even sparkling! The spectacle, equally repulsive and fascinating, proved irresistible: Those farther back in the line pressed forward for a glimpse, and the hubbub grew ever louder.

"What color's next?"

"Move! I can't see!"

"Green again—he must be starting over!"

"Pink! He didn't do pink before!"

The episode seemed to be going on rather longer than Raffa had intended. Had he made the emetic too strong? He fought the impulse to go to his friend's aid; having made his brave decision, Jimble would be aghast if he wasn't allowed to do his part.

Raffa had to take his chance now, while all the attention was focused on Jimble. He slipped into the Hall, unnoticed by the guards or anyone else.

CHAPTER TWENTY-TWO

FROM inside the entryway, Raffa cast an anxious glance back at Jimble, who now was looking even paler than usual, except for a smear of bright color around his lips.

Finished at last with his task, Jimble straightened and wiped his mouth. He caught Raffa's eye and gave him a valiant wink. Raffa was relieved: With luck, Jimble would be none the worse for their stunt.

They had timed their arrival for well before the start of the hearing. Trixin had told Raffa that the hearings chamber was at the end of the wide corridor to the right of the entrance. To the left, a smaller, ordinary door stood ajar. He took a peek inside. It was a long, narrow room, lined with benches. A sign on the wall read, WITNESSES MUST REMAIN IN THIS ROOM UNTIL DISMISSED.

He cautiously opened one of the big double doors and peered around it, ready to claim mistakenness if anyone was there. But the chamber was empty. Quickly he entered and closed the door behind him.

The chamber was a large room, its length at least twice its width. To the right, at the end of the room, was a platform set with a long table and three ornate chairs. For the Deemers, he thought.

On the floor in front of the platform was a large mosaic-tile rendering of the emblem of Obsidia: a brilliant red flower rising from three jagged cracks. The emblem symbolized how the land and its people had survived and rebuilt after the devastation of the Great Quake. Flanking the emblem were several rows of chairs neatly angled toward the center of the room.

To the left was a set of stairs, which led to the gallery overlooking the chamber. The gallery was for observers, but Trixin had said that audiences were no longer allowed at the hearings. Raffa would have the gallery to himself.

He climbed the stairs and ducked behind the barrier

in front of the first row of benches. Elaborately carved with narrow gaps between its moldings, the barrier would conceal him from those in the chamber below, as long as he remained in a crouch. He would be able to hear everything, and see the Deemers. Anyone seated in the rows of chairs would be facing away from him.

Raffa continued to examine the room from his higher vantage point. The floor was highly polished. Each chair had a cushion. It was a rich and elegant room—

Except for one thing.

Against the wall near the door stood a cell made of iron bars. The bars were black and thick. Raffa shivered; they looked as if they would be colder than ice to the touch. While tall enough for most men, the cell was both narrow and shallow. Anyone inside would have to stand, because there was no room to sit or even to turn around.

The cell was for the prisoner.

For Da.

Rectangles of light from the windows slanted on the floor. It's past sunpeak, Raffa thought. The hearing should be starting soon.

He prodded his cheeks and jawline. The swelling had already gone down considerably; he was probably recognizable now. He wondered if there was another way out of the Hall—a door that was unguarded. Why hadn't he asked Trixin? He fumed at himself: It seemed that he never quite thought things through all the way.

The double doors swung open. Raffa tensed and drew closer to the barrier, putting his eye to a gap.

Half a dozen tendants and complices filed in. They were followed by two men and two women wearing dark blue robes, who seated themselves in the chairs closest to the platform. Several more people entered; from their fine dress, Raffa guessed that they were Commoners.

A guard came in next. He waited until everyone was settled, then boomed out, "All heed! All heed! Prisoner enters!"

Raffa clamped his mouth shut to trap a shout of indignation. The guard's warning made it sound like Da was dangerous, or at the very least frightening. . . . Da— the levellest, most steadfast person in all of Obsidia!

Raffa shifted a little so he was at a better angle to see the door.

Two more guards entered, holding Mohan between them. His hands were bound in front of him.

Tears filled Raffa's eyes. His father, so familiar, exactly as Raffa remembered him—except dearer now, after the long months of separation and the terrible fear that he had been lost in the cabin fire.

With a pang so sharp it left him gasping, Raffa recalled how he had long chafed against his father—against Da's endless restrictions and overprotectiveness. In the last few months, Raffa had learned a great deal about being independent, and sure upon certain, it had been far more challenging than he ever could have imagined. He ached for the chance to go home with both his parents and try again for a compromise, knowing what he knew now.

Da! he wanted to cry out. *Da, I'm here!* He watched with his fists clenched as the guards put Mohan into the iron cell.

For the first time in months, Raffa was in the same room as his father. But locked inside that despicable cell, Da seemed even farther away than when Raffa had been in the Suddens.

One of the blue-robed men went to stand in front of the platform, off to one side. "Rise, please," he intoned.

Everyone stood as a door in the corner behind the platform opened. Raffa hadn't noticed it before. Two women and a man entered. They wore gray robes with an iridescent, silvery cast to the fine fabric. The justice symbol was embroidered on their robes above their hearts. The Deemers.

They sat in the three chairs. The woman who had taken the center seat picked up a small mallet and struck a miniature brass gong on the table. A surprisingly sonorous chime filled the room. She nodded at the man in the blue robe.

"Lawtender Ong, please begin the proceedings."

As everyone else sat down again, Ong turned so that one shoulder was toward the Deemers, the other toward the rest of the room. Raffa could now see his face.

"The Commons brings charges against Mohan Santana," Ong stated, "accused of arson, the deliberate act of setting fire to Commons property. Deemers Regnar, Zina, and Barogram sitting."

Everyone else in the room murmured a response: "So heeded."

Then Ong cleared his throat. "Deemers, your indulgence is begged for an alteration to the usual proceedings."

Deemer Regnar, in the center seat, tilted her head. "Yes?"

"Chancellor Leeds wishes to address the chamber."

The Chancellor!

Raffa inhaled sharply, then froze, afraid that someone might have heard him. No one turned his way, so he let out his breath slowly. He hadn't seen the Chancellor enter; she must have come in while he had his eyes on his father. Now she stood up from her seat in the second row and strode forward to stand on the emblem.

"Welcome and grace to you, Chancellor Leeds," Regnar said.

The Chancellor inclined her head. She wore a red tunic the exact shade of the tiled flower. Her silver hair was a striking contrast to her tan skin, and her bearing, while stately, also seemed quite relaxed and comfortable. She took a moment to glance around the room, then smiled at one of the Commoners.

Her smile was warm and friendly. How could someone doing such awful things have such a nice smile?

She turned to face the Deemers, and her expression grew solemn. "Noble Deemers," she said, "Lawtender Ong has already stated that the accused is charged with arson to Commons property. A crime against the Commons is a crime against Obsidia itself, the very land we all love so well. Because of this accusation, I and

Advocate Marshall and a number of Commoners have chosen to attend this hearing."

She sounds like she's hosting a party, Raffa thought with bitter resentment.

Seated among the Commoners was a tall man whose head was shaved bald, his scalp a shiny pale tan. Raffa saw that his high collar glinted with metal decorations. *That must be him—the Advocate*. Holder of the highest office in Obsidia.

"We are honored by your presence, Advocate," Regnar said. "Shall we proceed?"

The Chancellor returned to her seat while one of the guards fetched the first witness from the antechamber. The witness, wearing the uniform of a Commons guard, took his place on the emblem. Raffa narrowed his eyes. He couldn't be sure, but the man might have been one of the guards at the shed compound last night.

"Mannum Pelanade, you work as a Commons guard?" Lawtender Ong asked.

Pelanade was facing the Deemers. On hearing Ong's voice, he seemed confused. He turned to look at Ong, then back at the Deemers. "I'm a guard—that's right."

"And last night, you were on duty?"

279

"I was, yes." Again, he swiveled his head uncertainly.

"Where?"

"At—at my post." Pelanade rocked back and forth on his heels, obviously nervous.

"What is the location of your post, Mannum?"

Now Pelanade lifted his chin. "I can't say. Sorry. Sworn to secrecy. It's a secret."

Deemer Regnar frowned. "Mannum, this is a Deemers' hearing. You must answer the questions—"

The Chancellor stood again. "If I may, Deemer?" She did not wait for a response. "Mannum Pelanade is assigned to a project that cannot be disclosed at this time, for reasons of Obsidia's security. I myself vouch for the fact that he was indeed on duty at his post last night, and if you would like, I will summon his senior for confirmation."

So the project is still a secret, Raffa thought, even from the Deemers. He wondered who knew about it. The Chancellor, Senior Jayney, Mannum Trubb. Uncle Ansel, Garith, and Trixin . . . The guards and servients who worked at the compound obviously knew of its existence, but that didn't mean they knew how the animals were going to be used.

Who else? The Commoners? Raffa glanced down at

Advocate Marshall. *Does he know?*

The Advocate's job was to represent the people of Obsidia, while the Chancellor oversaw the execution of the laws of the land. Raffa was horrified to think that the Advocate might be part of the project. But it was equally horrific to think that he *didn't* know—that the Chancellor was using her power and position without the rest of the government's knowledge.

The three Deemers were conferring in whispers. Deemer Regnar spoke, her expression stern. "The witness may continue to testify without disclosing the location of his post," she said. "We are reserving judgment for the moment. We may require that fact to be revealed at a later time, if we deem it necessary."

"Thank you, Deemers," the Chancellor said, and sat down again.

Lawtender Ong continued his questioning. "Will you tell us what happened last night, while you were on duty?"

"Yes, 'course I will," Pelanade answered. "Suppose you don't want to hear about the ordinary things, like my rounds and that. Just the dis-ordinary? Like the fire?"

"That is correct. Will you please describe the fire?"

"Weren't a big fire. But a long one."

"A long one? What do you mean by that?"

Pelanade bent his arm and then extended it, as if pointing out into the distance. "Nice and straight. Followed the fence on one side of the gate, ran on from it on the other. Guess you could say it were two fires, not one."

"Could the fire have been an accident?"

Pelanade looked indignant. "No, Lawtender! Much too tidy. Someone put down tinder and such, so it would burn like it did."

Ong turned to the Deemers. "Mannum Pelanade had three colleagues on duty with him. All of them witnessed the fire. They can, if you wish, be brought in to testify. We requested Mannum Pelanade's presence because he alone saw the person who set the fire."

"I did," Pelanade said, puffing up with importance. "Me, I'm the only one who saw."

"Can you describe this person?"

Pelanade scratched his ear, then cleared his throat. "It were certain dark, y'know. Hard to see clear-like. . . ." His voice trailed off.

Raffa's hopes bloomed. *It's true! He couldn't see me clearly. Everything happened so fast—he can't possibly know who was there, he can't say for certain that it was Da!*

"So you're unable to give a description of the person you saw?"

"I was comin' in the gate, see, to fetch a shovel. And I saw someone the other side of the com—"

The Chancellor coughed very loudly. Pelanade stared at her for a moment.

Raffa drew in his breath. *He almost slipped up and mentioned the compound!* Clearly, the Chancellor had interrupted him deliberately.

Now it was Pelanade who coughed. "Er, I mean I saw someone across the—across from me. Weren't right next to me or like that. In the distance."

"Mannum Pelanade, I must ask you to think as hard as you can. Isn't it possible that you might have gotten a clearer glimpse of the person at some point?"

Pelanade seemed baffled by Ong's insistent tone. Ong waited a moment longer, then said, "Deemers, I would like to request a brief recess."

Deemer Regnar frowned. "Already? This is only the first witness."

Ong reddened a little. "I beg the Deemers' pardon.

We need the recess to—to check that certain preparations are in place. These will"—a pause—"ensure that there are no further delays to the proceedings," he finished firmly.

"Very well," Regnar said. "A quarter of an hour, Lawtender, no more." She tapped the gong.

The three Deemers rose and exited through the door behind the platform while a guard led Pelanade out of the chamber. To the witness room, Raffa thought. He must be the only witness, if they're not going to call the rest of the guards. No one else was at the compound.

The Chancellor rose and went to speak to another guard standing near the cell. He left the room, which was now rustling with quiet activity. Some people stood and walked about; others chatted with their seatmates. Raffa lowered himself to his bottom so he could stretch out his legs.

The Deemers returned, and the gong was struck. A guard escorted Pelanade back into the chamber. As Pelanade took his place before the Deemers again, the double doors opened. Yet another guard entered, along with a woman and two children, a girl around ten years old and a boy perhaps four or five. The guard had a firm grip on the woman's arm. She was looking around the chamber in confusion.

No, Raffa thought. She's not just confused. She's frightened.

"Da!" The little boy had spotted Pelanade and was trying to push past his mother, who clutched at his arm. "No, I want to go to Da!" he whined, struggling against her hold.

Raffa saw Pelanade's eyes widen in surprise—more than that, in *shock*—at seeing his family there. Then he looked at the Chancellor, and even from the gallery, Raffa could sense Pelanade's alarm.

"You're all right there, Nel," he said to the boy, his voice tight with anxiety. "Stay with your mam now."

Deemer Regnar spoke sharply. "Excuse me, Missum. I must ask you to leave. Audiences are not permitted at hearings."

"Y-your pardon," the woman said, her voice quavering. "There must be some mistake. They came and fetched us, but I don't understand why—no one told us—"

"Guard," the Chancellor interrupted, "please escort the missum and her children out of the chamber. The hearing must continue."

Raffa watched them leave, feeling as bewildered as the woman had looked. He could not shake the sense that something important had just happened—but what was it?

"Now, then," Ong said. "I will ask you again, Mannum Pelanade. Can you describe the arsonist?"

"Do better than that," Pelanade said, his voice rough with belligerence. He turned and pointed at Mohan in the cell. "Him—he's the one I saw!"

CHAPTER TWENTY-THREE

*H*E'S *lying!*

Raffa's world reeled. He closed his eyes against the dizziness, then opened them and looked through the gap at his father. Mohan's face was blank, his expression impossible to read.

Why was Pelanade lying now? *He was telling the truth before—that he couldn't see clearly. Why is he suddenly saying it was Da?*

Meanwhile, Lawtender Ong was making a pronouncement. "All heed that the witness has pointed out the accused. There are no more questions for this witness. He is hereby dismissed."

Pelanade could hardly leave the chamber fast enough. As the double doors closed, Raffa heard him calling out, "Nel! Nel, boy, come here to me!" His family must have been waiting outside the chamber.

Ong was speaking again. "Next witness. Senior Ansel Vale."

Raffa had sense enough not to gasp—just barely. He clutched the carved posts of the barrier as his uncle entered through the double doors. Ansel passed right in front of Raffa, who could see him much more clearly than he had from across the yard at the pother quarter. Slender, with fine features and wavy brown hair . . . Raffa had forgotten how much Uncle Ansel looked like his sister—Raffa's mother, Salima.

Ansel took his place on the emblem.

"Ansel Vale, how long have you known the accused?" Ong began.

"For at least twenty years. Since we were in our teens."

"What is your relationship? Are you friends?"

"Friends, yes. Colleagues—we often worked together. And brothers. I mean that literally—he's my brother-in-law, married to my dear sister."

"So you know him well."

"Yes." A pause. "Or perhaps I should say, I thought I did."

Raffa seethed at that response. "I thought I did"? What was that supposed to mean?

"Has the accused been a guest in your home?" Ong asked.

"He has," Ansel replied. "Off and on, these past few months."

Ong paused. "Was he at your home last night?"

Ansel shook his head. "He was not, Lawtender."

"Do you know where he was?"

"I understood that he was traveling. He was expected back today. I was surprised when he arrived at my home sometime after daybirth, I had not expected him so early."

"And you do not know where he was last night."

Another shake of the head. "I do not."

Raffa found himself trembling. On the one hand, Uncle Ansel was telling the truth, and Raffa could hardly fault him for that. On the other hand, he seemed to be casting doubt on Da, in slight, subtle ways.

In the hidden center of his heart, Raffa had been

hoping—no, he had been *assuming*—that one day, some way, somehow, he would be reconciled with his uncle. But every word Ansel was speaking now diminished that possibility. *He should be doing the opposite—he should be speaking up for Da!*

"You do not know where he was, but he was definitely not with you in your home."

"That is correct."

"Thank you, Ansel Vale. You may step down."

"One moment, please," Deemer Regnar said. "Lawtender, if the purpose of this testimony was simply to establish that the accused was not at Senior Vale's home last night, I must object to the waste of the chamber's time. We seek to know where the accused *was*, and specifically if he was at the site of the fire. Where he was *not* is of no relevance."

Ong bowed his head, visibly chastened by her words, then mumbled something inaudible. Raffa's eyes widened in relief and gratitude. It seemed clear now that Ong was grasping at smoke to implicate Da—probably at the Chancellor's behest. But at least for the moment, Deemer Regnar appeared to be out of their malicious reach.

Ansel went to sit in one of the chairs. Raffa saw his father's gaze sweep the entire chamber, from the Deemers to those seated, including Ansel and the Chancellor. Then Mohan looked up at the windows, the ceiling, the gallery. . . .

Raffa blinked. He could have sworn that Da's eyes met his for the merest of moments. But neither Mohan's face nor his body gave any sign of recognition or surprise. *I must have imagined it.*

"Next witness, please," Ong said. "Senior Salima Vale."

Raffa clapped his hand over his mouth to keep from crying out.

Mam!

The door to the chamber opened, and his mother entered. She was wearing a simple tunic, pale yellow. Raffa knew it well; he remembered helping her tint the fabric: Last summer, out in the back dooryard . . . a dye made of onion skins . . . stirring the fabric in the big basin with a stout stick . . .

He was puzzled that his mind should fix on those details at such a moment. Then he realized that it was a scene from home. *That's what Mam is. She's my home.*

Salima took her place on the emblem. Raffa didn't even want to blink; he was staring at her so hard that his eyes burned.

"What is your relationship to the accused?" Ong began.

Salima raised her chin. "He is my husband," she said, her voice clear and firm. "We have been married these fifteen years now."

"As married to the accused, you have the right not to give testimony against him. Do you invoke that right?"

"I do," she said in the same strong voice.

As the chamber buzzed and hummed at her response, Raffa's heart leapt. It was all he could do not to cheer.

"Salima Vale, by the same measure, you have the right to testify in your husband's favor. Do you wish to do so?"

A long pause. Then Salima lowered her head—and shook it.

"The witness must voice her response," Deemer Regnar said.

"No," Salima said, in a voice like a shadow. "I—I do not wish it."

Raffa's fist flew to his mouth as dismay flooded through his whole body. *She must have been with*

*him—she has to know that he didn't do it! Why won't
she say so?*

He wanted to throw himself down the stairs and
into his mother's arms. He wanted to hug her as tightly
as he could and at the same time, beat at her with his
fists. What reason could she possibly have for refusing
to speak on Da's behalf?

"The witness is excused," Ong said.

Salima joined those who were seated. Raffa noticed,
with a rawness burning his insides, that she sat in the
chair next to Uncle Ansel.

Raffa tore his gaze from them to look at Da. Mohan's
expression was unchanged; his eyes were on Ong, not
Mam.

Then his father raised his bound hands and covered
his mouth with one of them, as if he were thinking hard.
He leaned back so he was looking up at the ceiling, then
moved his head slowly from side to side. As he looked
to his left, he stared directly at Raffa, then patted his
mouth a few times. Finally he lowered his hands and
looked at the Deemers.

Stunned, Raffa could not mistake what he had just
seen: Da had secretly signaled him.

His hand covering his mouth. He was telling me to

keep my mouth shut! But how can he possibly know—

Raffa thought of the conversation with Trixin that morning. *She had talked to Garith. And Garith said he'd told Da and Mam that I was in Gilden, and that I was going to the secret shed compound.*

Da could not know everything that happened last night, but he seemed to have assumed—rightly—that Raffa was somehow involved.

"No further witnesses," Ong announced.

Regnar said, "Mohan Santana, you now have the opportunity to defend yourself. What have you to say?"

Mohan held his head proudly but said nothing.

"Do you deny the charges?" Regnar asked.

No answer again.

Raffa could barely keep still. First Mam, and now Da himself! What was the matter with them—had they both gone daft? *Someone must have seen you last night—tell them! Why aren't you defending yourself?*

Then realization stung him so hard that he almost jumped: *He* wants *to be convicted! He's going to take the blame so that I'll be in the clear!*

"In accordance with the rules of this chamber," Ong said, "because the accused does not deny the charges, the Deemers need not pass judgment. It is hereby determined that the accused is guilty of arson—"

"WAIT! DA, NO!"

Raffa leapt to his feet. Every head turned his way.

"It wasn't him! I'm the one who did it!"

The sibilance of voices grew to a buzz as Raffa rushed down the gallery stairs and was immediately pinioned by a guard. He could hear Mam's voice calling him. Deemer Regnar rang the gong over and over, shouting for order.

When at last the noise began to subside, Mohan was the first to speak.

"Deemers! I cannot fathom the reason for my son's falsehood. Perhaps he wishes to be a hero."

"So you are now prepared to confess to the crime?" Lawtender Ong said.

"I am," Mohan said.

"Da!" Raffa cried out. He struggled against the guard holding him. "He didn't do it, I swear to you! I'll tell you exactly what happened! The sheds—"

"Silence him, guards!" the Chancellor shrieked. "Take them both to the Garrison, by my command!" Her face and her voice were distorted by fury.

A hand was clapped roughly over Raffa's mouth and

nose. He tried to bite, but the guard was wearing thick gloves. Raffa gagged, barely able to breathe.

"Please, no!" Salima's voice, begging. "He's only a child!"

Raffa stopped struggling, and the guard loosened his grip enough to allow a breath. Salima had risen from her chair in an effort to reach him, but Ansel gripped her arm, holding her back.

He saw, too, that the Advocate seemed unmoved. His head was tilted, his eyes oddly unfocused.

Deemer Regnar struck the gong again. "Silence in this chamber!" she ordered, her voice like iron. Then she stood. Raffa saw that she was quite tall; standing on the raised platform, she towered over everyone in the room.

"Chancellor, with respect," she said sternly, "the Deemers are independent of your office. You have no standing to give orders in this chamber!"

The Chancellor's face smoothed out in an instant. "Deemers, your pardon," she said, her voice completely calm. "In cases of more than one confession, is it not the law that all who confess be held until the facts can be established and guilt correctly assigned? We have just witnessed two different people confessing to the same crime."

Regnar was silent for a moment. "That is correct," she said at last. "But again I register my objection. Within these walls, it is my colleagues and I who command the guards and deem as needed."

"Your pardon again," the Chancellor said. "I apologize sincerely." She bowed her head over her joined hands.

With a nod, the Deemer sat down again. She and her colleagues conferred again in whispers. Deemer Barogram addressed Salima.

"Salima Vale, what is your son's name?"

Salima replied without taking her eyes off of Raffa.

Then Regnar tapped the gong again. She waited until the chime had faded away completely.

"We deem that Mohan Santana and Raffa Santana be held in the Garrison until one week from today, when a hearing will be held to determine their guilt or innocence. We hereby close this session."

Raffa saw the anguish on his mother's face as he was taken away. The guard kept his hand over Raffa's mouth and marched him from the chamber and out a side door into the lane, where one prison wagon was waiting and a second just arriving.

He realized at once what this meant: that he and Da would not be put in the same wagon. He would have no chance to speak to either of his parents.

Not since the discovery of his family's destroyed cabin had Raffa felt such despair. The guards took away his rucksack and his rope, which made him feel even more powerless. He slumped in a corner of the wagon's cell, his head buried in his arms, for the entirety of the bumpy ride. He could not even rouse himself when he heard the Garrison gates squeal open.

The wagon creaked to a stop. A guard opened the door. "On your feet," he ordered.

As Raffa stumbled away from the wagon, he glanced around the Garrison's courtyard. Months earlier, he had been here, in this exact same spot. With Trixin and Kuma's help, he had managed to flee, slipping away from a handful of guards with the aid of a few botanical concoctions and a timely intervention by Echo.

This time, there was no one to help.

Raffa felt himself shrink and shrivel as he was led through a door and down a flight of stone steps. The walls were stone, too, menacing in their thickness and solidity. At the bottom of the steps was an iron barricade; beyond it, a long dark corridor lined with cells.

He was shoved into one of the cells. The door slammed behind him. He held his breath, listening hard, but he heard no further noise or activity. It seemed that Da was being put into a separate wing: They were making sure to keep father and son well apart.

The cell was all but dark. A lantern in the corridor shed a wan light that barely reached beyond the barred opening in the cell door. Where the walls met the ceiling, there were some chinks in the stonework, letting in a few forlorn slivers of daylight.

Raffa saw a pile of dirty straw in one corner, a bucket in another. The damp walls bore a slimy coat of mold. Odd scuttling noises disturbed the dank air. He had heard rumors of the rats in the Garrison, some supposedly the size of cats. . . .

He shivered, missing the familiar warmth of Echo against his chest. What would the bat do when Raffa didn't return to the storeroom? *His eyes are getting blacker. . . . Maybe he'll leave now and go back to the wild—and I won't even have a chance to say good-bye.*

He thought his heart would surely break into little pieces if that happened. How much more miserable could things get?

He was surprised to hear a screech of rusty metal

as the barricade to the cells swung open. Raffa spun around and grabbed the bars of the door.

Let it be Mam, he pleaded with all his might. *Please let it be Mam.*

A single set of footfalls, too heavy and ponderous to be his mother's.

A figure rounded the corner.

The light from the lantern fell on the bearded face of Senior Jayney.

CHAPTER TWENTY-FOUR

RAFFA'S legs almost gave way beneath him; he clung to the bars to stay upright. He was furious with himself for the fear surging through him and was determined not to let Jayney see it.

"I know about the attack on the settlement!" Raffa shouted. "Why are you targeting Afters?"

Jayney was so surprised that he actually stumbled.

Raffa was exultant: Going on the immediate offensive had worked!

But the small victory shrank away with Jayney's first words.

"Where is the bear?"

Fear roiled up again in Raffa on hearing that voice—lazy and laconic, but somehow all the more menacing for that.

Raffa pushed himself away from the bars and went to stand in the corner, with most of his back to Jayney. He crossed his arms and leaned against the wall in a posture of defiance.

"Where is the bear?"

Silence. Raffa was still shaking; he hoped that Jayney couldn't see it in the dim light.

"Tell me where it is, and I will see to it that both you and your father are freed and cleared of all charges. What a fine and dutiful son you would be!"

Raffa kept his body still, but his mind twitched and trembled. That was what he had wanted—to save his father from a prison sentence.

Maybe he could lie. He could tell Jayney that Roo was somewhere else, in the Forest of Wonders, or the Suddens.

No. The Chancellor was not stupid. She would surely order Raffa to guide the expedition to recover the bear, and would not release Mohan until the bear was back in Gilden. If Raffa led the searchers astray, it would go far worse for both himself and Da.

Jayney made a noise that sounded like a growl. "You and your stubborn father," he said. "Your mother is the only one of you who sees sense."

Raffa stiffened. What was he saying about his mother? *"Aunt Salima has been working in the laboratory. . . ."* Those were Garith's words. Raffa hadn't thought anything of it at the time, but what Jayney had just said made him realize that his mother must be working alongside Uncle Ansel.

Could she be helping with the dreaded project? Was that why she had refused to testify in Da's favor?

Raffa doubled over, nearly sick at the thought. *No, Mam, no no no . . .*

"I will give you a few days to reconsider," Jayney said. "Your cooperation would be advisable. It would be much less pleasant for both of us if you have to be . . . forced to respond."

Torture. He's talking about torturing me.

Raffa had a brave, foolish vision of himself withstanding physical pain, refusing to answer, no matter what they did to him. He straightened up and tried to look impassive. Jayney was still speaking.

"I'm told that you were at the hearing. Well, then, you saw how little it takes to bring about the desired result."

The hearing? What was he talking about?

Jayney was watching him closely. After a moment, he said, "Mannum Pelanade has a lovely family, don't you think?"

With those words, the shiver that had chilled Raffa in the hearings chamber returned with twice the strength, like a lump of ice thrust down his throat. *They forced Mannum Pelanade to lie! All they had to do was show him his family. If he hadn't said what they wanted him to, they would have done the family harm somehow!*

"Oh, good. I can see that you understand now," Jayney said, like a master pleased with an apprentice. "And another thing to remember: A house is but a building. It can be replaced, rebuilt. Even better than before."

Raffa could make no sense of the sudden change in subject. Why was Jayney talking in riddles?

"Not so with people," Jayney went on. "A father, especially, is irreplaceable."

Jayney's meaning struck Raffa like a blow, and he collapsed onto all fours like an animal.

He's talking about the cabin—they're the ones who

burned it down! And he's saying that . . . just like with Pelanade, if I don't tell him where Roo is, they'll torture Da, not me—

"Think about it, young Santana," Jayney said, his tone as light as if discussing a picnic. "I will be back in a few days for your decision."

As the sound of footfalls faded, Raffa put his face in the filth of the cell floor and wept.

A night and a day passed. Raffa's awareness of time came only from the narrow stripes of sunlight that reached the cell floor from the windows of the stairwell. He dozed for brief, fitful snatches of time, in constant fear of the rats.

At one point, a silent guard opened the cell door just enough to shove in a bowl of muddy gruel and another of water. Otherwise, Raffa had no contact with anyone. The darkness and loneliness made him feel as if he were going mad.

Jayney's threat hovered over his thoughts, lurked under them, circled endlessly. Tell the truth about Roo, enabling the Chancellor to recapture her—and force her to become a terrible weapon? Or refuse to answer, dooming Da to unimaginable torture?

If only he had a way to get a message to Kuma! *Then I could tell Jayney about the gorge, but Kuma could move Roo somewhere else before he gets there.*

No matter how long and hard Raffa racked his brain, he could not think of a way to reach Kuma.

The only break in his dread of Jayney was the thought of the second hearing that loomed ahead. If he confessed and gave details of the fire that only he knew, the Deemers would surely sentence him for the crime, and Da would go free.

But the sentence would be a term in the Garrison. A term of *years*. How would he endure it?

I can't. I can't!

He retched in terror. When the spasm passed, he thought, *If I let him, Da will take the blame and I'll be released.*

Shame overcame him before he had even finished that thought. *But I have to tell the truth! I can't let them sentence Da instead!*

The fear and the shame alternated in his mind until he was dizzy. His time in the Garrison already felt like an eternity—yet it was passing all too quickly toward Jayney's return. Where was Mam? Why hadn't she come to see him?

He tried desperately to cheer himself by thinking of his friends. Garith, Kuma, Trixin, Jimble . . . Did they even know where he was? Maybe Kuma had reached Gilden by now. Maybe she had gotten together with Garith, and they were planning to—to—

To what?

To stop the project, he told himself doggedly. He hoped with all his heart that his efforts at the compound had not been completely futile. At Kuma's settlement, foxes and stoats had been a vital part of the attack. Raffa had released a shedful of each: Would that be enough to delay an attack on the slums—on people like Davvis and Jimble's other friends, whose lives were already a struggle?

Raffa slumped on the pile of soiled straw. He was not asleep, but not truly awake either; numbness was his only refuge.

A tiny noise from a corner of the cell. He tensed. Something was moving about there. Another rat? He dragged himself into a crouch, ready to swat or kick if anything touched him.

He waited, hearing only the sounds of his own breathing. Then—a pinch on his shoulder! He jerked his head violently, but before he could slap the creature away, he heard a familiar, beloved squeak.

"Ouch!" Echo said.

Raffa cried out, a wordless sound of pain and joy and despair and relief. He cupped Echo in both palms close to his cheek, sobbing so hard that he almost choked.

"You found me!" he gasped between sobs. "You came back to me!"

Echo gave a little shake and began to groom himself. "Water," he said.

Raffa sniffled, then gulped and hiccupped as his sobs began to ebb. "Are you thirsty, Echo?"

"Not thirsty," the bat replied. "Rain."

Was it raining? It had been dry when Raffa was last outdoors, which now seemed like years ago.

"Salty," Echo said. "Raffa eyes, rain salty."

"Rain salty—oh. Oh, that's what you mean." He put Echo on his sleeve so he could wipe his eyes. "Yes, Echo, I was—my eyes were—raining salty. It's okay, I've stopped now, see?"

His smile was small and shaky, but how good it felt to smile! Raffa had no idea what would happen next, but he knew one thing sure upon certain: His journey with Echo could not end here, in a squalid, hopeless cell—he simply would not allow it. Whatever the road ahead, he swore from the depths of his heart that they would travel it together.

"How did you find me?" Raffa asked in wonder.

"Talk Jimble, find Raffa," Echo chirped.

So they *do* know where I am, he thought. He stroked Echo, and the warmth of the bat's tiny body seemed to spread from his fingertip through his whole being. "I'm sorry I got your fur wet," he said softly.

"Raffa good."

"Echo good."

Echo had brought more than just comfort.

He had given Raffa hope.

ACKNOWLEDGMENTS

I am grateful to Cece Bell, for her immediate and gracious response to my request that she read the manuscript of this book and comment on the depiction of Garith's deafness. Any errors that remain are entirely my responsibility.

Many other people supported me during the writing of this book, including:

Team HarperCollins, especially my editor, Abby Ranger.

Ginger Knowlton, Marnie Zoldessy, and everyone at Curtis Brown, Ltd.

Julie Damerell, always my right arm and often my left, too.

Steve and Vicki Palmquist at Winding Oak.

Writer and illustrator friends, and other colleagues from the book world: If you're wondering whether or not I mean you, the answer is yes. You are my community.

Steve Mooser and Lin Oliver. The volunteers at SCBWI, RACWI, and We Need Diverse Books (an entire herd of alpacas to the incredible Publishing Internship Committee). All those working to connect young readers to books, with a shout-out to the dedicated teachers and librarians.

My extended family, especially Ed Park, Craig Park, and Anna Dobbin. Extra hugs to Callan and Hattie for lighting up my days.

Ben, my left midfielder.

And a special note of thanks to fans of the first Wing & Claw book: I'm so glad you love Echo as much as I do. Your enthusiasm inspires and sustains me.